CHAPTER ONE

THE FIRST THING JAKE MEYER noticed about her was the same thing everyone else saw: two delicate wrists wrapped in white gauze. Seated one table over from him, a young woman drank a small espresso and nibbled at a croissant. Though Jake tried not to stare, his eyes kept drifting back to those fragile, bandaged wrists.

The autumn sun shone bright enough to give the appearance of summer, but a slight chill to the air betrayed the changing season. The café's outdoor seating was full of locals and tourists alike taking advantage of the opportunity before everything was taken down for the winter.

The waiter came to his table and Jake ordered, annoyed at himself for pointing at his selection in the menu as he used his German.

"*Eine Melange, bitte*," he said. His German was passable, but he couldn't hide his American accent. He noticed the woman at the table next to him look over briefly.

"Anything else, sir?" the waiter asked in clear English.

Jake was never certain if this was an attempt by the Viennese to be helpful, dependent as they were on tourist dollars, or if it was a slight show of superiority. *Your German is awful, let me use my English instead.*

"No," Jake answered in German. "That is all."

The waiter left, and Jake watched the traffic pass. It was late morning and the streets were full of locals, with only the occasional tourist, map in one hand, camera in the other. Although Café Strauss sat just a block or two away from the neo-Gothic beauty of the Rathaus, or city hall, few tourists wandered off their prescribed paths.

Jake glanced over at the table next to him and caught the girl looking his way. He smiled broadly, overcompensating for his awkwardness at seeing her bandages—not that she was trying to hide them. She looked back to her coffee, but not before giving him the slightest of smiles.

Now that Jake wasn't focused solely on her wrists, he thought she looked familiar. She was probably a bit younger than him, with long blonde hair that was loosely tied back. Her features were delicate, but with a lingering bit of baby fat still in her cheeks. She was almost certainly a fellow student, either at the University of Vienna or the nearby Medical University.

Although a few of Jake's lectures were large, with nearly one hundred students, he felt confident he didn't have any classes with the young woman. More than likely, he'd passed her in the halls or seen her sitting in the *Mensa*, the German term for a student cafeteria.

The waiter brought his coffee and set it before him. Vienna was a beautiful city in many ways, but to Jake it was the coffee culture that made this place one of the best in the world. What the Viennese call a *Mélange* is really nothing more than a cappuccino with a pretty name, but it somehow tasted better here.

He thanked the waiter and sipped his coffee. This was where the true majesty of the Viennese café came into play. If he wanted, he could now sit here all day long with this one coffee. He could read the newspaper, gossip with friends, or just watch the clouds drift by. Even if he never ordered a single additional item, there would be no pressure for him to leave and give up his valuable table. Jake appreciated this little bit of indulgence, so different from the constant rush of his native country.

He felt good this morning. The sun was shining, he didn't have a class until late afternoon, and his coffee was amazing. He might even order a second one today. His positive thoughts were interrupted by a glance at the woman next to him, staring blankly into the distance. More than the bandages, she looked sad. Painfully solitary. He felt he should attempt some friendly conversation, and waited until she noticed his look.

"*Guten Morgen*," he said, knowing she almost certainly spoke English, but a friendly "good morning" in the local language was always a safe bet.

City of Ghosts

by

Shawn Kobb

ISBN 978-1514803530

Dedication

For my mother.

She gave a slight start, not expecting interaction. "*Morgen*," she muttered in return.

She didn't seem too eager for conversation. He returned his focus to his coffee and watching a pair of nearby pigeons peck at invisible bits of food on the sidewalk.

"My name is Anna," she said after a minute. Her English was good, but with a noticeable accent.

Now it was his turn to be caught off guard. She was looking at him, more quizzically than truly friendly, perhaps wondering why this strange man had decided to speak to her. Certainly she was pretty enough to have solicited awkward attempts at conversation in the past. Looking at Anna now, however, Jake wouldn't have been surprised to learn it was her first time ever speaking at all. She had an air of childlike innocence, but her eyes were haunted. It was also possible he was simply reading too much Victorian-era literature for class, he reflected.

"Hi. I'm Jake."

She nodded, as though his name was obviously so. She looked back to her coffee and, for a moment, he thought the brief encounter was complete. He was debating whether to try and further it when she took the next step.

"Are you a tourist?"

He didn't want to be offended. There was nothing wrong with being a tourist. He had traveled extensively around Europe and was obviously a tourist himself at times, probably just as oblivious as the crowds he complained of in Vienna. Still, it always stung a bit when locals assumed he wasn't from here—though it was certainly true. It made him feel he was somehow failing at living in Vienna.

"No, I live here," he said. "Well, I moved here a few months ago. I'm going to uni here."

Again Anna nodded. Jake thought it might be more of an affectation. It made her appear agreeable. The pause was awkward and he rushed to fill it.

"Are you a student?"

"Yes. At the University of Vienna."

"What are you studying?"

"Biology."

"To become a doctor?" Jake asked.

She scrunched her face, for a moment confused by his question. "I will receive my diploma," she said. "But I will work in a lab."

Much of the academic vocabulary was different here, Jake remembered. Due to the high quality and nearly cost-free nature of education, there were many people here with advanced degrees. He didn't know for certain, but probably most of the students at the University of Vienna were going for a doctorate of some kind, but not all would become medical doctors working with patients.

"Do you have a specialty?" he asked, uncertain whether his terminology made sense.

"It is, I think you say 'genetics'?" She pronounced the word with a hard *g*.

"Genetics," he said, correcting her. "Very interesting. I'm studying—"

He cut himself off, distracted by an immovable shadow that had fallen over her. A young man stood at the other side of her table, facing Anna. He had an athletic build and blond hair that framed a strong jaw and piercing eyes. The man looked down at Anna with concern. She didn't appear surprised to see him, but neither did she seem that happy.

He spoke to her in German more rapid than Jake could follow. Jake could tell by his air alone that what the man said was important—or at least he thought so. Anna had returned to her distracted air. During their brief discussion, Jake had forgotten about the telltale bandages at her wrists, but this brought it back.

He felt he should interrupt, in case she didn't want this man here. By the look of the guy, Jake was really hoping Anna wouldn't ask for his help in getting away from the man. He looked quite a bit tougher than Jake felt.

"Anna," Jake started.

The man looked down sharply at Jake, but Anna spoke before he could say anything.

"Jake, this is my friend Christian."

For a moment, Christian looked truly wounded by the term *friend*, but quickly regained his composure. He changed his mask of concern and anger to a smile and looked at Jake.

"It's nice to meet you," Christian said, his English pronunciation very good. He turned back to Anna as though Jake's role here was finished. Perhaps it was.

He switched back to German and again Jake couldn't catch it all, but it was obvious Christian was demanding that they talk. His voice sounded pleading, desperate, but Anna clearly had no interest in the conversation. She barely looked at him, her gaze fixed on her now-empty cup of espresso.

Christian continued to try to get through to her as others at the café looked on—some discreetly, others less so. The waiter watched from the doorway, appearing to weigh whether he should step in before business was affected.

Jake was uncertain what he should do. He didn't know Anna, but should he step in? Was that what a gentleman would do? In America, that is what one would do, right? Christian didn't seem threatening, though. It appeared to be a simple lovers' spat, but the bandages on Anna's wrists told a darker story.

Just as Jake had made the decision that he must speak up, Anna spoke quietly, but sharply. It was German, but this Jake understood.

"You lie," she said. "And I am finished with everything."

Christian looked wounded. Jake could see the poor man's heart breaking. He appeared ready to try again, but reconsidered and suddenly turned and walked off. The café returned to business as usual.

Anna watched him walk away. She opened her mouth and for a moment Jake thought she would call after the man. Her shoulders dropped and she looked down at her coffee before turning to Jake. She gave him a false smile.

"I am sorry. It was very nice to meet you this morning, Jake."

With that she stood, left a few euros on the table, and walked away quickly.

"Anna. If you want..." She kept walking, not acknowledging him.

CHAPTER TWO

JAKE'S APARTMENT BUILDING STOOD ON a quiet street in the ninth district of Vienna. It was a nice part of the city, and many of the buildings belonged to either the University of Vienna, the Medical University, or the enormous General Hospital, the largest hospital in Europe.

His building was typical for Vienna—an *Altbau*, or pre-WWII-constructed stone building with a beautifully decorated facade. His apartment was on the third floor. There were a few other rentals in addition to his flat, as well as a tailor on the first floor. Like many of the buildings in the area, most of the residents were university students.

There was no elevator and he walked up the old stone steps, his hand trailing along the wooden railing topping the decorative iron banister. Reaching his apartment, he keyed himself inside and found his roommates in the midst of a typical conversation for them.

"You are an old lady at the age of twenty," shouted Helmut. He was red in the face and nearly out of breath. "Life is wasted on you and, honestly, I think you are doomed to a life of solitude and boredom."

Mira sat in her favorite chair in the corner of the room, seemingly unaware of Helmut's rant. She held a book in front of her—Jake could make out only the words "history" and "civilization" in the title—and continued her reading.

Helmut quickly pivoted from apparent anger to cajoling.

"One little drink, Mira. We will be gone an hour, at the most. I need a break. Please…"

Mira noticed Jake standing in the doorway, placed her hand in her book to mark the page, and rested it on her lap.

"Good morning, Jake," she said.

"Am I interrupting something?" Jake asked.

"Jake," Helmut said, walking to Jake's side and dragging him by the arm toward Mira. "Please, tell her that there is more to life than studying? Tell her that she will die alone and unhappy if she doesn't take a break and go to the café with me."

"Mira," Jake said dutifully. "Helmut would like me to inform you that you shall meet a terrible fate if you do not have coffee with him."

"Please do not encourage him. I have to study, and I can make coffee here."

"It's not the same—" Helmut started before she cut him off.

"And some of us are in Vienna to actually complete our degrees."

The three of them had been roommates for the last two months, their arrangement facilitated by a program at the university. Despite the scene before him, Jake considered himself lucky. The three of them got along remarkably well. They were three foreigners in a foreign land, all enjoying Vienna—albeit in their own ways.

"Let her read in peace, Helmut," Jake said. "The day has barely started. I'm sure Mira will go out with us later for a drink."

Mira raised an eyebrow at Jake, but otherwise said nothing. He thought he detected a hint of that rare smile at the corner of her lips.

"It's agreed, then," Helmut said, clapping his hands together. "Tonight, we drink."

Jake suspected he and Mira were in silent agreement that this was a battle for later in the day. It was just as likely that Helmut would become distracted by something else and forget all about going to the café.

Jake went to his bedroom and dropped his bag on the floor. He had a German language class in the afternoon, and hadn't done any studying yet. Shouldn't simply living in a German-speaking land count as homework? Unfortunately, his professors didn't agree and his rather slow progress in the language appeared to support their point of view.

He sat on his bed and opened his MacBook. He could hear Helmut in the living room still talking about the amazing evening they were all going to have. Helmut was quite capable of maintaining a conversation with himself as long as others in the general vicinity grunted their occasional acknowledgement.

Jake checked his email, but didn't have anything of interest. Flipping over to Facebook, he read the posted highlights of friends and relatives back in the States. He felt increasingly detached from these people, and wasn't sure why he even bothered. They had all moved on with their lives. His friends were getting married. A few even had children on the way, and almost none were still in school.

When he'd graduated high school, Jake had announced to his parents that he was going to backpack around the world using his savings. They had objected and thought it reckless, but couldn't stop him. His six-month planned trip eventually stretched into one year, and then nearly two before the money ran out and he returned, convinced he should enter college.

Everything had been a mess since then, and Jake wondered whether it would have been better if he'd never returned to Ohio. He feared his reappearance after so much time away had been the gasoline that finally ignited the smoldering blaze he had left behind.

Mira's cell phone rang in the next room, a bit of Shakira's "Hips Don't Lie" filling the flat—further indication that beneath her librarian's exterior was a fun-loving girl. As she answered, Helmut appeared in the doorway.

"The uncle," Helmut rolled his eyes. "I don't want to listen to that. She turns so submissive on the phone with him. It crawls me out."

"Creeps," Jake said as he pulled a German textbook out of his backpack. "It creeps you out."

"Exactly so!" Helmut said. "And you don't need that book. You've got the pure source of German right before you."

"Somehow I think the words I learn from you won't help me pass my exam."

"My mother is from Hanover, Jake," Helmut said. "That is true German. Here you will only learn *Austrian* German." Helmut gave an exaggerated shiver.

They switched to German. On Jake's side, this obviously simplified the nuance of his conversation considerably, but it was good practice and he had to admit that Helmut was surprisingly patient with Jake's abuse of the German language.

Jake attempted to explain what had happened at the café that morning. Helmut asked a question that Jake didn't understand, but it was clear after Helmut pantomimed cutting his wrists.

"Yeah," Jake said. "I mean, I guess it could have been something else, but between her mood, the fight, and the bandaged wrists, I'm not sure what else it would have been."

"Well, you're lucky she left when she did," Helmut said. "You do not want that type of drama. Trust me on this."

"I'm not sure I was even interested," Jake said. "I mean, she was pretty, don't get me wrong, but there was something about her that made me want to know more. Maybe my psychology classes are starting to draw me to troubled souls."

Helmut laughed. "In that case, you have two prime subjects in this very flat."

"Very true. You two alone should be enough for me to earn my PhD."

"Me?" Helmut asked with feigned shock. "I'm the only sane one here!" He bellowed with laughter, as though his joke couldn't have come off any better.

CHAPTER THREE

JAKE LIED TO HIMSELF AND said Café Strauss had the best coffee in Vienna, or at least his neighborhood. That was the only reason he returned at the exact same time for the next three days. Certainly that reason, and no other.

On the third day, he sighed and paid the waiter.

"Excuse me," Jake asked in German. "Do you remember the young lady who had the argument here a few days ago?"

The waiter's face scrunched with an almost comical look of concentration.

"She was blonde, and another young man showed up and they argued?" Jake said.

"Ahh, yes!" the waiter said at last. "With the *Verbände*?"

Jake didn't know the word, but assumed it meant bandages. He nodded and pantomimed wrapping something around his wrists.

"No," the waiter said. "I think I have seen her here before, but I do not know her name. So many dramatic young students." He laughed as though Jake could understand. Honestly, he could.

Jake thanked the man and headed toward class. It was Thursday and he had Fundamentals of Psychotherapy, one of his more interesting classes. The professor, like many of the teaching staff, had not only a strong academic background, but a professional one as well.

His lecture hall was housed in an oddly modern building of glass and steel, in direct contrast with the intricately carved stone facades in the rest of the neighborhood. As he turned to enter, he stopped at sight of a familiar face. Her blonde hair hung loose today, but there was no question who it was:

Anna.

She was dressed casually, a backpack bulging with books slung over her shoulders. Her hair whipped about in the wind. The bandages on her wrists appeared to have been changed and were smaller now, so the wounds were obviously starting to heal. Jake thought it interesting that she wore nothing to hide them. Putting on his amateur psychologist hat, he suspected that meant either a call for attention or a detachment from common societal norms.

She looked straight ahead and, if she noticed or remembered Jake, she gave no sign. As he approached, he stepped in front of her and slight annoyance crossed her face.

"Anna? It's nice to see you again."

She smiled politely, the expression appearing far from genuine. Along with it was a look of complete non-recognition.

"I'm sorry," she said. "Where have we met?"

"Café Strauss. A few days ago?"

She blushed slightly in embarrassment, remembering the scene.

"You took off before I had a chance to really introduce myself," Jake said.

"I was having a very bad day. After the scene Christian caused, I couldn't handle sitting there and enduring the stares."

"It's no problem, I understand," he said without really meaning it.

"Well…" Anna said.

She stood stiffly, occasionally brushing a stray hair from her face. Anna glanced past Jake, in the direction she had been heading. *I can take a hint*, he thought.

"It was nice to see you again," he said. "I wish I could talk more, but I have to get to class."

"Yes, me as well."

"I have a few classes in this building, so I'm here quite a bit," he continued. "I'm sure we'll run into each other again sometime. Maybe we can do coffee again."

He felt like a desperate loser as the words came from his mouth, but he was helpless to stop them. He wasn't even sure he was attracted to her—not to mention that everything about her seemed to be a red flag warning any sensible person away: probable suicide attempt, an upset ex-boyfriend, her general disinterest in him. Even with all that, he was drawn to her. He felt an urge to protect her, to help her through the troubles she obviously faced. Given a similar scenario in class, he'd say it was a classic case of White Knight Syndrome.

"Yes," Anna said. "Maybe. It was good to see you again, Jake."

She didn't wait for an answer before continuing on her way. She only made it a short distance before she was stopped again. This time it wasn't Christian, the ex-boyfriend, but an older man.

He was probably in his late fifties, with salt-and-pepper hair and a neatly trimmed beard of the same color. He had distinguished tortoise-shell glasses and an air of pretension about him. Add a tweed jacket with patches on the sleeves and his picture would be next to "professor" in the dictionary.

"Anna," he said, gently grabbing her by the elbow. "I'm glad to have caught you before you left."

Jake pulled his phone from his pocket and pretended to be deeply engrossed in it, using the excuse to linger and eavesdrop. The interaction was odd, but it took him a moment to understand why. Typically, relationships between students and teachers in Austria were more formal than they were in the States. In the U.S., it was common for students to be on a first-name basis with their professors, but here—particularly with the German language—it was much more formal. For this man to call Anna by her given name was quite unusual.

His German was clear and easily understandable, with the slightest hint of an accent that Jake couldn't place.

"I was hoping you could stop by my office," the man continued. "I would like to discuss your thesis."

"Is there a problem with it, Herr Professor?" Anna asked.

"No, nothing like that. But I have some suggestions that I believe could strengthen your research and make for a better result. I am quite busy today, but I could stay late if you would like to stop by."

"I don't want to bother you outside of normal office hours," she said.

Jake saw her eyes darting around a bit. With Jake, she had been distracted and slightly aloof. Now she seemed almost childlike, a toddler caught with her hand in the cookie jar. Anna held the straps of her backpack tightly, her back rigid as though ready to run.

"You know it isn't a problem, Anna," the professor said. "Shall we say six p.m.?"

He took a small notebook from an inner pocket, flipped to a page, and began to write. Anna's eyes locked on Jake, still standing before the entrance of the building. He looked down and frantically started mashing buttons on his phone, the screen blinking quickly between random apps as he launched and closed them.

"Actually," Jake heard Anna say, "tonight is no good for me. I am meeting my friend here for dinner."

That caught Jake's attention. He looked up and saw she was pointing at him. The professor turned to face Jake. He felt like a frog about to be dissected under the man's steely gaze.

"Herr Professor Schmidt," Anna said, moving closer. "This is my friend…"

"Jake Meyer," he said, saving her. Jake extended his hand and the professor took it. The older man's grip was strong, his hands oddly smooth.

"Jake," Anna said, smiling broadly at him. It was the first time he'd seen her show her teeth. The smile looked out of place. "This is Herr Professor Rudolph Schmidt. He is my advisor."

"It is nice to meet you," Jake said in German, suddenly aware of every one of his linguistic shortcomings.

"You are American?" Schmidt asked. It was phrased as a question, but sounded like an accusation in Jake's ears.

"Yes, Herr Professor. I'm from Ohio originally, but I've been in Vienna a few months now studying at the university."

Schmidt's eyes continued to bore into Jake.

"Perhaps we can meet tomorrow instead?" Anna asked. "I will stop by your office and make an appointment with your secretary. Thank you for the kind offer to help."

He turned away from Jake and back to Anna. The professor's face relaxed and he looked kindly once more.

"It is no problem. It is not only my duty, but my pleasure."

Anna grabbed Jake by the arm and started to pull him away, both from Schmidt and the academic building. There was no way he was going to make his class on time now.

"It was nice to meet you," Jake called while being dragged away. Schmidt gave the slightest of nods, but Jake got the idea the feeling was not mutual.

After they rounded the corner, Anna finally stopped and turned to him. "I am very sorry about that," she said. "He is a good man. A brilliant man, in fact, but sometimes I worry…"

"That he has a crush on you?" Jake finished.

She looked puzzled. "A crush?" she repeated, obviously unfamiliar with the American term.

"Sorry. That he is interested in you. Romantically?"

Anna sighed. "Yes," she said. "I'm afraid that may be true, and I'm not sure what to do about it. He is my academic advisor. I must work closely with him in order to bring my studies to completion. I have seen him be very critical of students' mistakes in class. I can only imagine how he would be if I rejected him."

"That's a tough situation," Jake said. "Still, you'll have to confront it eventually. I'm not sure how many dinners we can go to before he starts to get suspicious."

Jake said it jokingly, but clearly Anna feared he had misinterpreted her excuse. He probably had. Her previous mask of distance and sadness slid back into place.

"Yes," she said. "You are right. I was just caught off guard this time. I will talk to him tomorrow and attempt to set some boundaries."

"I actually am free for dinner if you'd…"

"Weren't you going to class? You will be late." Anna turned quickly and walked away. After a few steps, she stopped and looked back at him. "Thank you again for your help."

So much for riding to the rescue.

CHAPTER FOUR

TESS MCINTOSH SIGHED AND ATTEMPTED to refocus her attention on the young Indian man standing in front of her. Between them was nearly an inch of bullet-resistant glass—not bullet *proof*, as her colleagues had been quick to point out on day one. While it made her feel quite safe during the occasional unpleasant visa interview, it did nothing to improve the already-terrible communication between applicants who often spoke poor German or even worse English, and herself.

She keyed the button to the microphone, waited for the crackle to dissipate, and tried again.

"I'm sorry, sir. I don't understand. Why have you decided to renew your American work visa in Austria instead of your home country of India?" *Or anywhere else but my window*, she added silently to herself.

"Yes," the man answered. "That is true."

Tess took a deep breath. It would be funny if she didn't have forty more interviews to get through this morning.

"I know it is true, sir," she said, speaking slowly and clearly. "I know you are here. What I want to understand is why you left the United States and chose to come to Vienna in order to renew your work visa. Do you have family here? Are you on vacation here?"

"Yes," he said, smiling.

She tried to remind herself how lucky she was to have Vienna as her first international diplomatic assignment as a Foreign Service Officer. Most of her cohorts were dealing with similarly challenging visa applicants, but in places like Nigeria, Saudi Arabia, or the Mexican border. She would receive no sympathy from them.

She gave up on her current course of questions and looked over his paperwork, doing her best to ignore his smiling face pressed against the glass, his forehead leaving a greasy smear. Everything was in order, and it appeared he had been a model employee for a small technology firm in Florida. She still didn't know why he'd chosen to renew his visa in Austria, but there was nothing saying he couldn't. She did a final check in the various immigration and criminal databases on her computer. It came back clean, no indication of trouble with U.S. law or immigration authorities. She looked at the notes from his last visa interview, which had been recorded two years earlier. Valid job. Qualified. Clean record.

The last thing to pop up on her screen were the results from the scans that had been run through fingerprints and facial recognition software. Nothing strange.

Tess typed up her notes and added them to his record. She slid a small ticket to him under the glass.

"All right sir," she said. "Your visa is approved. It will be ready tomorrow. Come back after two p.m., and bring this ticket with you. You will receive your passport then. Have a nice day."

His head bobbed side-to-side as he grinned. She remembered one of her colleagues that was headed to Chennai mentioning this peculiar bit of body language. It was their version of agreement. The man turned and walked away.

"I've got a project for you, Tess," said a man's voice right behind her.

She nearly jumped out of her seat.

"Jesus!" she said before she could stop herself.

She turned to see her supervisor standing there, no hint of a smile on his face. Come to think of it, she couldn't recall ever seeing any sign of a smile on Thurston's face, but maybe it was only hidden by his ridiculously bushy mustache. Along with the facial hair, thick glasses, and dark tie with short-sleeved white dress shirt, he was the very model of a middle-management drone from 1987.

"I've got a project for you," he repeated, as though she hadn't heard. Apparently nearly wetting her pants had not been sufficient proof that she had.

"Sure. What's up?"

He placed a Post-it note on the counter next to her, the stickiness mostly gone from the back, the corner peeling up immediately. On it was written in his tidy handwriting, "Jacob Meyer," plus a phone number and address in Vienna's ninth district.

"Welfare-and-whereabouts check. His parents called Main State and they contacted us. They can't reach him and want us to have him call home."

"How old is this kid?" she asked.

"Twenty-something, I guess. He's supposed to be a student at University of Vienna. Just get him to call home and we can be done with it."

That's embarrassing, Tess thought to herself. She wasn't much older than him and was serving her country as a diplomat abroad. This guy's mommy wanted him to call home. *There's got to be some issues there.*

"Should I do it now?"

Thurston leaned past her to peer through the window. Most of the seats were full of waiting visa applicants. Although he wasn't a terrible boss, he wasn't exactly the mentoring type and her adjustment to her first consular tour abroad had been a game of learning by trial and error.

"Maybe we should just send all the visa applicants home so this guy can call his mother?" Thurston asked. She could tell his question was rhetorical. "Finish up and do this in the afternoon."

Tess felt her cheeks burning, but worked to keep her anger in check. Mr. Meyer wasn't the only one who was being treated like a child. She nodded and turned back to her window. Grabbing the next passport on the pile, she turned on her microphone and called the name.

CHAPTER FIVE

THREE HOURS LATER, TESS sat at her desk with a tuna fish sandwich and a bottle of sparkling water she'd bought from a kiosk across the street. She wasn't normally one to work through lunch, but the amount of visa applicants lately had all of the consular officers putting in more hours than usual. Although the number of foreigners in Vienna seeking American visas was relatively low, so was their staff. Combine this with a large number of U.S. tourists managing to lose passports, get arrested, or die, and the consular section stayed quite active.

As she picked at her sandwich, she ran a quick Google search on her welfare-and-whereabouts case. Unfortunately, Jacob Meyer was a bit too common a name for anything definitive. She tried to look him up on Facebook—purely for professional reasons, of course—and although a dozen or so people by that name popped up, none had Vienna listed as their location.

None of this was entirely necessary, as the guy's mother had already provided a phone number. Then again, if it was a good number then why couldn't his parents reach him? The most likely reason was that he didn't want to talk to them.

It wasn't her job to play family therapist, but it wasn't uncommon for consular officers to find themselves acting as parents to people far older. Although Tess was still new on the job, some of her colleagues had the craziest stories about their encounters with Americans around the world. Even Thurston, normally not one to trade anecdotes with the staff, had a hilarious tale about the time he'd had to allow a destitute woman to use his home shower before the local airlines would permit her to board the airplane home.

Performing a W&W check was one of many duties the American Citizens Services section of a U.S. Consulate provided. What concerned mothers, fathers, boyfriends, wives, and long-lost uncles failed to understand was that while the consulate would do its best to find the person, there was no requirement for that person to agree to talk to whomever was attempting to find them. There is nothing illegal about cutting off ties with your family.

If Tess could manage to track Mr. Meyer down and he told her he wanted nothing to do with Mom and Dad, all she could really do was call Mom and tell her that her son was alive. Anything else was protected by privacy laws. It might make him a bad son, but as long as he was mentally competent and not a threat to himself, there was nothing more she could do.

She picked up the phone and called the number. She could tell from the ridiculously long string of digits that it was a cell phone.

It picked up after one ring.

"Hello?"

A man with an American accent answered in English. A good clue, Tess thought.

"Hello," she said. "I'm trying to reach Jacob Meyer. Is this him?"

"Yes…"

"Mr. Meyer. My name is Tess McIntosh and I'm a consular officer with the American Embassy. We were contacted by a woman named Judith Meyer, who says that she is your mother and that she has concerns for your well-being." For a moment, there was silence on the other end of the line. "Mr. Meyer?"

"You have got to be shitting me," the young man said at last. He didn't sound angry as much as exasperated.

"I promise I'm not. I take it Judith Meyer is, in fact, your mother?"

"That's her, all right. I can't believe she called the embassy. I'm really sorry."

"That's fine," Tess said.

"No," the man said. "It really isn't."

"It's what we're here for. She says she's been trying to reach you for the last two weeks with no luck."

"I've just been swamped lately at school. If she doesn't hear from me, she gets a bit freaked out. It's…" he hesitated. "Well, it's a long story and nothing you care to hear. Listen, I'm really sorry. I'll make sure she doesn't bother you guys again."

Tess switched to a more casual tone. "Honestly, it's not a big deal. I have a mom who worries about me, too. To her, any foreign country is automatically dangerous. Even Austria."

"It's not quite like that. It's…drama. Don't worry. I'll call her."

"That would be great. Listen, Mr. Meyer—"

"Please call me Jake."

"Jake," Tess said. "I need to call your mother as part of my job, but you can tell me how much I'm allowed to say. What would you like me to tell her?"

"Did she say anything else?" he asked.

"Anything else? I don't think so. What do you mean?"

For a moment the phone went silent. It was clear Jake was struggling to come up with his response. Although she knew her mother really did worry about her, Tess was suddenly grateful for the genuine lack of emotional drama she had in her family life.

"Jake?"

"Please just tell her you spoke to me. I'm fine, and I'll call her soon."

"No problem," Tess said. "That's what I'll do."

"Thank you for your time on this. I'm sure you've got other things to worry about."

"It makes for a nice break from interviewing Austrian students about their travel plans."

"Sounds real exciting," he said. After a moment he added, "Sorry, that sounded patronizing."

"Yeah," Tess laughed. "It did, a bit."

"I guess I never really thought about who works in the embassy. So, you interview students? That's why you got picked to call me?"

"I interview everyone. These days, it just happens to mostly be students arranging for visas to study in the States next year."

The inevitable awkward silence followed. *That's what you get for chatting up a total stranger, Tess.*

"Well, It was nice talking to you," Jake said.

"You too," Tess said. "And Jake? Everything is okay, right?"

"Honestly," he said. "It is. Don't let my mom's paranoia worry you. You focus on the true crazy Americans here."

"Will do. Please let me know if I can be of any help in the future."

She didn't even know why she'd said that. No sane consular officer would go out looking for more people to help. It was tough enough to keep up with the true emergency cases. Maybe being single and overseas was starting to get to her a bit.

"Thanks again," Jake said, and hung up.

CHAPTER SIX

JAKE COULDN'T BELIEVE HIS PARENTS had called the American Embassy. He was an adult, for God's sake. Still, he felt like a jerk. There was a reason he was five thousand miles away from his little Ohio town and all the drama that came with it, but of course his mother worried.

Jake paid for his bratwurst at one of the little *Würstl*, or sausage, stands that were ubiquitous throughout Vienna. He took a large bite as he thumbed the "Home" icon in his phone's contacts. Jake was still chewing when his mother answered after the first ring.

"Jake?"

She couldn't understand his muffled reply and he forced the food down as quickly as he could.

"Sorry, Mom. I'm eating, and on the way to class."

"Why haven't you called? I've left messages."

"I know. I'm sorry. I've just been busy. My abnormal psych class is kicking my…butt."

"Jakey," she said. "Don't be mad, but when I didn't hear anything from you—"

"…you called the embassy," he finished for her. "Yeah. They reached out to me. You really didn't need to do that. Everything's okay. Honestly."

She was silent a moment too long. Jake knew she was trying to keep herself together. She hated crying in front of him. Now he felt like an even bigger ass for taking so long to call her.

"We met with the school's lawyer again yesterday."

Jake's face flushed. "What do they want now? More bullshit waivers?"

"Jakey," she said.

He nearly stepped in front of a passing Vespa and knew he needed to calm down. His mother had enough to deal with. He didn't need to make her feel worse about it.

"I'm sorry, Mom. I just wish they'd leave you alone."

Again the silence was a beat longer than Jake liked to hear. "No, it's okay," she said.

Ahead of him loomed the massive main building of the University of Vienna, its white facade gleaming in the strong afternoon sun. Between the telephone conversation and attempting to not get run down while crossing the busy streets, Jake didn't notice the commotion near the school until he was almost on top of it.

"Jakey," his mother said. "Did you hear me?"

"I'm sorry, Mom. Can I call you back later?"

There was clearly something wrong. The crowd was moving about like ants who'd just had their home demolished by a toddler. A police car pulled up as he approached.

"Is everything all right?" his mother asked.

"Yeah. I'm just running late for class." It took almost nothing to worry her these days; the white lie was justified. "I'll try and give you a call later."

"Okay. Don't work too hard."

~

Jake worked his way through the crowd. Just a few feet from the front of the building was the crumpled body of a man. Jake instinctively looked up, and saw a window along the top floor hanging open, nearly four stories above the concrete sidewalk below. For a moment there was a flash of blonde hair as a young woman stuck her head through the window and looked down at the scene below. The brief glimpse was all Jake needed to know who it was: Anna.

She quickly withdrew back into the building, and Jake thought at first he may have imagined it was her. It was quite a ways up and, with the bright sun, difficult to see. She had been on his mind. Had it really been her?

A girl about his age in a plaid coat burst into tears, and a student Jake recognized from his psych class comforted her. A blond-headed officer shouted in German, signaling the crowd to move back. Sirens got louder as more emergency responders descended on the scene.

Jake focused on the body lying in the center of the crowd. It was face down, but clearly that of a young man. There was surprisingly little blood on the ground, apart from a small pool near the face. One leg was twisted at an odd angle under the other, and he could see the sharp white of bone coming from a forearm where the man had clearly made an instinctive yet futile attempt to use his hands to break his fall.

Jake circled through the quickly growing crowd to get a better look at the man's face. In addition to curious and upset students, tourists were also being drawn away from the U-Bahn stop across the street. He noticed more than a few taking photos, some making no attempt to hide their callous actions.

As he managed to maneuver through the crowd and push his way back to the front, he finally could see the man's face. It was splattered with a bit of blood and one eye stared straight ahead, while the other was closed as though in some sort of garish wink.

It was Christian. The boyfriend—or ex-boyfriend—of Anna. The man he had just met a few days ago, who had argued with her so publicly.

For a moment, it felt as though Jake's heart stopped. The animal part of his brain immediately connected a series of information bytes into one story, but his more rational brain couldn't believe it could be true. Jake looked again to the open window high above. There was no one there, but he knew what he had seen. It had been Anna. He knew it.

The argument, Anna appearing in the window above, and now Christian's mangled corpse before him. What had happened? He had to find her.

Medical personnel were now present and pushing a gurney toward the scene. They crouched near the body as more police arrived to keep people back. Jake used the movement of the crowd to skirt the edge of the circle toward the doors. They were propped open as more and more students and faculty came from the building to see what had happened. At this point, more people were leaving the building than entering, and Jake struggled to move.

The excited chatter of German surrounded him, and it was impossible for his agitated brain to process it just then. He realized some in the area were actually asking him if he knew what had happened. He could only look at them blankly, and they quickly turned to someone else nearby for answers.

Jake was working his way through the rapidly growing crowd, desperate to get inside the building, when he saw Anna. Her blonde hair caught the sun as she pushed herself to the front of the circle to see. The medics lifted Christian's body onto the gurney and Anna's hand went to her mouth, the white bandage still around her delicate wrist.

For a moment, her mouth formed a perfect O of shock. Jake watched as that shock turned to fear, and she quickly glanced around—for what, he couldn't say. Her eyes darted past him, but if she saw him, she gave no indication.

"Anna!" Jake shouted.

Anna whipped her head toward the sound of his voice. He saw her mouth form his name, puzzlement creasing her brow as though she couldn't conceive of how he could be here.

Jake started to push through the crowd again, trying to make it the last twenty feet to get to her side.

Anna seemed to understand his intent, and shook her head. Jake noticed, but didn't understand. Suddenly she pulled back from the police officer in front of her and also began to move through the crowd, away from him.

Jake called to her again, but if she heard she made no attempt to stop. He lost sight of her as they both fought through the still-growing crowd. As he made it to the far side of the circle and onto the clear sidewalk nearby, there was no sign of Anna.

Jake jogged down the road, but couldn't find her. People continued to move past him, eager to find out what had happened. It was hopeless. Anna had disappeared, leaving Jake confused and her boyfriend dead on the sidewalk.

CHAPTER SEVEN

JAKE WALKED THE QUIET SIDE streets home, his mind still reeling with what he had seen. Anna had seen him. He knew it. She must have. Why had she run? Had she seen Christian fall from the window? *Who said he fell?* Did he jump? He'd seemed upset the other day about the break-up, but was he suicidal?

What if someone pushed him? Jake was surprised he went there so quickly. But if it was true, if someone had pushed Christian out of that window, then what did that mean for Anna? Had she pushed Christian to his death? Was she capable of such a horrible act? He barely knew her, but his gut said no.

If the bandages on her wrists were any indication, Anna was a troubled soul. Add to that the confrontation she'd had with Christian at the café the other day, and theirs clearly hadn't been a simple relationship. *I guess that would be putting it mildly*, Jake thought to himself. He wasn't sure what he had seen at Café Strauss earlier in the week. An argument, sure, but things didn't seem so dire that Christian would have committed suicide. Still, if Jake had learned anything over the last two years, it was that you never really knew what was going on in someone else's head.

How many times had his father grumbled about the "phase" his sister Lucy had been going through? She hung out with the wrong crowd. She liked the wrong boys. She dressed inappropriately. Jake had defended Lucy, told his parents to let her live her life and to make her own mistakes. A day didn't go by now that Jake would give anything to go back and do it all over.

He thought he should search for Anna, but didn't know where to start. He didn't know where she lived; didn't know when or where her classes took place. If she had a job, he didn't know what it was. The more he thought about it, the more he realized he didn't know anything about her, apart from her name and a few bits of story he had created in his head.

As he turned the final corner toward his apartment, a bigger question came to mind: why should he even care?

Looks? She was attractive, for certain. Anna may not have been the most beautiful girl he had seen in Vienna, but she could turn a few heads. Was that all it was? He was lonely here and, although he got along well with his roommates, he could only share so much with them. He desired a closeness that in his current life he didn't have.

He was so lost in his thoughts, Jake nearly walked right past the front door of his building. He'd barely realized he was walking home, but was glad when he reached the familiar steps. He had to talk to someone about what he had just witnessed, and his flatmates—Helmut in particular—would love the drama.

Inside, he dropped his bag near the front door. Helmut sat at his normal chair in the corner, papers and books strewn about him. He had a mechanical pencil in his mouth as he scrubbed a paper clean with a gum eraser. When finished, he glanced at the clock and then looked up to Jake.

"You didn't do the shopping yet?" Helmut asked.

"Shit," Jake said. "I totally forgot it was my turn. I've had a crazy afternoon."

"Right..."

"Seriously," Jake said. "You remember the girl I told you about—Anna?"

His only response was a blank stare.

"The blonde with the...?" He motioned to his wrists, not wanting to say it.

"Oh, Anna!" Helmut said. "Yes, I remember her. Did you have a hot date?"

"Not exactly," Jake said.

He recounted what had happened, pausing only to answer Helmut's questions and wait for his gasps. Helmut was one of those guys who was so animated it made every story Jake told feel like a masterpiece. With an incident as bizarre as Christian's apparent suicide, Jake almost forgot how damned depressing and strange the entire situation was.

"I need to find her, Helmut," Jake said. "Problem is, I don't have any clue where to start. I thought you guys might have an idea. Where's Mira?"

"Our beloved Serbian was in a particularly foul mood this morning. We screamed at each other a bit over coffee, and then she decided she needed some air. She went out for a walk. That was probably two hours ago."

"What did you do to set her off this time?" Jake asked, tired of feeling like he was the father of someone his own age.

Helmut's face took on an air of exaggerated shock and hurt. "Nothing," he said. "At least, nothing out of the ordinary."

Jake raised an eyebrow.

"Seriously. I didn't do anything. She came out of her room ready for a fight. I may have pushed her knobs…"

"Buttons," Jake said. "Not knobs. That sounds a bit dirty."

"Sorry, push her *buttons*," Helmut continued. "But I didn't start the fire, as your American poet Billy Joel once said."

Jake liked Mira a lot, despite her often stormy personality. Much like himself, Mira was an outsider. She had moved to Vienna from Serbia three years ago, mainly to go to school. Her uncle had immigrated to Austria many years back, after the war in the Balkans, and Mira's family decided she would have better opportunities here. Although she was quite independent, her uncle did check in on her from time to time.

"Don't worry," Helmut said. "She'll show up, as friendly as ever."

"Anna?" Jake asked.

"No, Mira. I don't know about your little mysterious nymph."

"Please don't call her—"

"If you want to find her, though, I'd head over to the registrar's office and see if you can get an address out of them. If nothing else, they'd probably give you her class schedule."

CHAPTER EIGHT

WITHIN AN HOUR, JAKE returned to the scene of Christian's death, not out of morbid curiosity but because Helmut's idea had been a good one and the registrar's office was in the same building as the accident. The crowd, along with Christian's body, was now gone. A few police officers stood about talking. Jake noticed the window above was now closed.

He walked inside and found a small reception area. Next to it was a board with classrooms and offices listed. None of it was much help to him, as he had little idea what—or even if—Anna studied in this building. A young man sat at the desk. He had a laptop open in front of him and appeared to be working on homework.

"Excuse me," Jake said. "Do you happen to know if Anna is here?"

"Anna who?" the student said without looking up.

"I don't actually know her last name. She's pretty, with blonde hair..."

"I don't think I can help you."

"She has bandages on her wrists," Jake added.

That was enough to at least make the student look up from his work.

"I don't think I've seen anyone like that around. Sorry."

Jake kicked himself for not knowing at least Anna's last name. He had no idea how he was supposed to find her again. He turned to walk away when he realized that, although he may not know where she'd gone, he did know at least one place she had recently been.

He turned back to the guy at the desk, leaned in, and said quietly. "What's with the police out front?"

"You didn't hear?" the student worker said, now eager to share in some gossip. "Someone jumped from the top floor earlier. *Splat,* right on the sidewalk out front. I was working when it happened, but by the time I heard the noise and looked up, he was dead."

"Any idea who the guy was?" Jake asked.

"I heard he was a student, but I didn't recognize the name."

"Seems like kind of an odd place to decide to kill yourself," Jake said, to himself as much as the worker.

"*If* he killed himself, you mean," the student added with a conspiratorial whisper.

"Could it have been an accident?" Jake asked.

"Maybe," the student said drawing out the word as though it was unlikely. "But I heard the police talking to each other about the possibility he could have been pushed."

It made sense that if the thought had occurred to Jake, it was certainly something the police would also be looking into. He really needed to talk to Anna and see what had happened.

He thanked the student for his help and continued into the building. Not being entirely certain from which floor he'd seen Anna poke her head out the window, he bypassed the elevator and took the stairs. Like many of the university facilities, the building was quite old. The stairs were wide and the stone was actually worn down in the middle from countless footsteps over hundreds of years. Despite the age of the building, because of its clever design and modern updating, it was well lit. Beams of sunlight shone through large windows and bounced off the white marble interior.

He was winded by the time he reached the fourth floor, but he felt sure this was the correct level—if Anna had been any higher, he couldn't have made out her face so clearly. He looked around for any indication of where to go. He walked toward the front of the building and found there were no classrooms on this floor. It seemed to be primarily offices.

The doors of all the offices along the front of the building were closed, but each had a small sign identifying the inhabitant. From up here, it was impossible to tell which office corresponded with the window he'd seen from below. He had thought the police might be up here investigating, but if they had, they had already finished their work.

About halfway down the hall, Jake stopped at an office that he thought could be the one where he'd spotted Anna. The sign next to it read, "Herr Prof. Rudolph Schmidt." Below it was an unfamiliar German word that Jake assumed must be a division or title.

"Schmidt," Jake whispered to himself.

Just as he remembered why the name sounded familiar, the door opened and he stood face-to-face with the professor Anna had introduced him to a few days ago. Anna had told Jake of her misgivings about Schmidt and now just a few days later, her ex-boyfriend jumps from the same professor's window? There was no way it could be coincidence.

Schmidt's lip curled quickly to a frown at the sight of the young man standing before him. He said something in German at a machine-gun pace that Jake couldn't begin to follow.

"Can I help you?" Schmidt repeated in English.

"Sorry," Jake said. "No, I was just looking for someone, but I don't see her."

"Don't I know you?" Schmidt said. "Are you one of my students?"

"No, I'm a psychology student, but I'm friends with Anna. I thought she might be here."

"Anna Duerning?" Schmidt looked immediately suspicious.

"Yes, and I..."

"You are her friend from the other day. I remember now. Why would you believe she would be here?"

"I didn't know for sure, but..." Jake wasn't sure how to finish.

"She is not here," Schmidt said. "In fact, I haven't seen her in a few days. She has missed my class. I'm not pleased by it."

"I'm sorry to have bothered you, Herr Professor," Jake said, backing away.

"If you see her, tell her to contact me," Schmidt said.

Jake nodded, turned, and quickly went back down the stairs. He glanced back once as he turned the corner to see Schmidt standing in the doorway of his office, watching him.

CHAPTER NINE

JAKE WALKED HOME, DEJECTED at his failure to find Anna. He was certain the window he had seen Anna poke her head from must have been Professor Schmidt's office. It also had to be the very same office window that Christian had fallen from. But if that was true, Schmidt must know. The police must have spoken with him.

Why would all three of them be in the office before Christian's death? Or, if Schmidt hadn't been there, why would Christian and Anna be there without him? The pieces just didn't fit.

A lovers' triangle? It seemed ridiculous, but Jake knew that crazier things had happened. Professor Schmidt had seemed far too casual with Anna the other day. Clearly she had wanted to get away from him—she'd even used Jake as an excuse.

Was Schmidt the other man? He was old enough to be her father. Hell, he was old enough to be her grandfather. Still, Jake knew that some women were drawn to the older, intellectual type; the sort of man who discussed Goethe and sipped brandy. Jake was more of a *Simpsons* and Guinness man himself.

It was none of his business. He didn't really know Anna. He didn't know Christian or Schmidt at all. He had his own problems—for one, his worried parents were asking for the U.S. government to track him down. If he didn't call home regularly, he was liable to see black helicopters hovering overhead.

Dropping his keys on the table inside the apartment door, Jake could see Helmut sitting in his usual chair in the corner.

"Mission was a complete fail, Helmut," he said.

"Ah, Jake?" Helmut said.

"What's weird is who I did manage to find. You'll never guess."

"Jake, you need to—"

"Guess whose office is on the top floor?"

The corner of the room was blocked by the edge of the dining room wall. Behind it, a woman's voice answered.

"Herr Professor Rudolph Schmidt," said the voice.

Jake came around the corner, unable to process what was going on.

"Anna!" She sat at the table, a cup of coffee beside her.

"Hello, Jake."

"What are you doing here? How do you even know where I live?"

"I'm sorry I ran earlier," she said. "I was frightened, and at that moment I just couldn't bear to talk to anyone."

She was pale, her eyes puffy as though she had been crying.

"I've been looking everywhere for you," Jake said. "How did you find my apartment?"

"I called the university registrar's office and told them you were sick and I had homework assignments to drop off. They gave me your address without any trouble."

Jake saw Helmut's smirk.

"A brilliant idea," Jake said. "I should have thought of it myself."

Helmut laughed.

"What is so funny?" she asked.

"Nothing," Jake said. "Ignore him. What happened? I'm very sorry about Christian."

Anna's eyes welled with tears at his name. Her normally peaceful, almost resigned expression started to crumble. She looked away from them for a moment and sniffed, trying to hold her composure. Jake looked to Helmut helplessly. After a moment, Anna turned back to them.

"We were finished," she said. "I think we both knew that, though he was having more trouble with it than I was. Still, I loved him."

She was quiet. Jake waited, thinking there must be more coming, but Anna didn't seem willing to volunteer anything further.

"What happened to Christian, Anna?" Jake asked quietly. "Were you there when he jumped?" *Please say he jumped*, he thought. The alternative was too terrible to contemplate.

For a moment he thought she wasn't going to answer, the memory still too raw. She took a drink from her cup, her hands trembling. She rested the coffee in her lap.

"I wasn't there," she said quietly, looking down at her coffee. "I don't know why he did it."

Jake didn't know what to think. She had been there—he'd seen her. He was certain he had seen her poke her head from the window. He could only think of one reason to lie.

"Anna—" Jake said.

Before he could finish his thought, the front door opened. Mira came in and walked straight to the living room. Jake had never seen her in such a state. Her brown hair, normally pulled back without so much as a strand loose, floated about her head as though she had just gotten up from bed. Her clothes, usually simple but fashionable, were unkempt, her shirt half-untucked. She looked as though she had been crying.

She stood at the edge of the room, processing the faces in front of her. Locking eyes with Anna, she jerked as though physically struck.

"Mira?" Jake asked. "Is everything all right?"

For a moment she didn't answer, and only continued to stare at Anna. Then, she looked down at her hands and seemed to notice her shirt was untucked. She adjusted it carefully, smoothing the front with trembling fingers.

"Yes," Mira said. "Everything is fine. I'm sorry. I just have had a bad day."

"You think you've had a bad day," Helmut said. "You can't imagine what else has been going on."

"Helmut," Jake said, noticing Anna start to tear up.

Helmut seemed appropriately embarrassed. He turned and awkwardly patted Anna on her knee. She didn't acknowledge it, but continued to stare into her coffee.

"I'm sorry, Anna. I just meant, we should be grateful for what we have." Helmut said. His voice drifted off, as though his justification sounded weak even to his own ears.

"Mira," Jake said, trying to change the subject. "This is my friend Anna. A close friend of hers sadly died today. I'm afraid we are not very good company at the moment."

Jake saw Mira's eyes harden—an odd reaction, he thought. She appeared to be holding back words. Mira was always something of an enigma, but this was odd behavior even for her.

"Anna, this is my other roommate, Mira."

"It is nice to meet you, Mira," Anna said. She stood and offered her hand to the other woman.

Mira hesitated a moment, but took Anna's hand and gave it one quick, perfunctory pump before dropping it.

"Yes," Mira said.

If Mira's rudeness bothered Anna, she hid it well; Anna seemed too distracted by her own grief and the trauma of the day to notice the odd behavior. He decided to ignore it. Let Mira come out and tell them if something was bothering her—there were more important matters to think about right now. He noticed Helmut staring at Mira, obviously also noticing her strange attitude.

They locked eyes, and Jake gave a subtle shrug.

Jake decided to continue the conversation where they'd left it before Mira had walked in.

"Why would Christian have jumped from that window? Had he been depressed?"

Anna failed to meet his gaze and looked at the floor, picking at an unseen speck of fuzz on her pants.

"I don't know. I do not think he was depressed, but he had been acting very strangely for a few weeks now. It is why we broke up."

Mira let out a huff of breath that was impossible to ignore. Anna, along with the men, looked to her. Anna's cheeks flushed with heat.

"Excuse me," she said. "Have we met?"

"No, you do not know me." Mira stared Anna down and said after a moment, "But Christian was my friend. He would *not* have killed himself. I know he wouldn't have."

The last words came out in a sudden rush. Mira seemed surprised herself at her outburst. Helmut and Jake spoke at the same time.

"Mira, what is wrong?" Helmut said.

"What do you mean you—" Jake started.

Anna cut them both off. "How did you know Christian? What do you know of his death?" She took a step forward, as though she would rip the answers from Mira.

"I..." Mira said. "I don't know. He should not have died. He deserved better than this."

She looked at Anna, and Mira's eyes flashed with heat. Mira took a sudden step toward the other girl. Her shoulders were pulled in tight and Jake could see the tendons of her neck standing out against her tan skin. She opened her mouth, but snapped it shut without saying anything.

Helmut and Jake looked on with shock, while Anna merely looked confused. Helmut stepped forward and grabbed the Serbian woman by the arm in case she was about to go after Anna, but Mira's anger melted as quickly as it had erupted. Her eyes filled with tears, something Jake had never seen happen in their time living together. She shook Helmut's hand from her arm and moved quickly toward her room.

"Leave me alone!"

She slammed the door of her bedroom and left the others standing confused. Helmut followed her to her door and tapped on it lightly, but Mira didn't answer.

Jake put his arm around Anna's shoulders. She didn't seem angry as much as confused and frightened. He could understand the confused part—he was feeling a little of that himself. Jake didn't know how all this drama had suddenly descended on his life.

"Maybe we should go for a walk? Give her some space, and I'll try to figure out later what is going on."

Anna nodded and they quickly left the apartment, where Helmut still stood at Mira's door gently calling her name.

CHAPTER TEN

TESS DROPPED THE HEAVY DUTY-officer bag on her kitchen counter. She grabbed a citrus-flavored beer known as a *Radler* from the fridge, pulled the duty phone from her bag, and settled in front of the television.

It had been a long day at work and, to top it off, she was starting her week as duty officer. U.S. embassies are twenty-four-seven operations; that means all staff have to take turns handling the after-hours calls that come in. Actually, the U.S. Marine Security Guard standing at the primary guard station known as Post One takes the calls, but he then passes them on to the officer on duty. For this week, that was Tess.

Although duty work in Vienna was pretty easy compared to places like Bangkok or Tijuana, it still left Tess feeling edgy and nervous. Just knowing that the phone could ring at any time during the night and not having any idea what or who could be on the other end of the line made it difficult for her to sleep.

Her last shift had been about five months ago. Overall, it had been quiet, with just a few American citizens calling in to report they had lost their passports. That was an easy one: *Come into the consular section the next morning.* There wasn't any way she could replace that herself in the middle of the night and, despite what tourists might think, a lost passport was almost never an emergency.

The only interesting call last time had been an arrest. For some odd reason, people who might be perfect law-abiding citizens back in the States got overseas and suddenly thought local laws failed to apply to them. It was ridiculous what people would do when traveling. Getting busted with drugs or prostitutes was most common, but fighting, trespassing, and public drunkenness were also high on the list.

The citizen Tess had been contacted regarding had been overjoyed to hear that someone from the U.S. Embassy had come to visit him after his arrest. Unfortunately for him, this enthusiasm quickly waned upon learning that Tess was not there to get him out of jail. He'd broken the law, and now he had to suffer the consequences—the same as any other person.

All she was there to do was to ensure the American was being treated equally to any Austrian arrested. She also offered to contact someone back in the States on his behalf, and she provided a list of attorneys. Too many movies had confused the general public about what diplomats were able to do.

Now, Tess scrolled through her Facebook newsfeed on the iPad, reading bits of life from friends, many of whom she hadn't seen in person for years. She also read about some of the adventures of her Foreign Service colleagues, now scattered around the world.

A sudden, shrill ring went straight through her. She suppressed a groan.

"Son of a bitch," she mumbled to herself.

If she was getting her first call within an hour of starting her shift, this could be a very long week. She grabbed the phone and answered it.

"U.S. Embassy duty officer," she said, trying to sound official. "This is Tess."

"Ma'am, this is the Marine at Post One. I have a call for you from the hospital."

Great, she thought. The hospital either meant an injured American or a dead one. Neither was going to be much fun. She looked up at the clock. It was just after seven p.m.

"Thank you. You can put them through."

The doctor at AKH, the enormous general hospital in Vienna, explained that an older lady had passed away while on vacation. They had already been in touch with the family back in the States, but the family had requested the embassy identify the body for legal and insurance purposes.

Wonderful. She wondered how eager people would be to go identify the body of a loved one in the morgue. They seemed more than willing to volunteer a stranger to do it for them. Still, she tried her best to remember it wasn't always all about her.

She thanked the doctor for his call and told him she would be there shortly. It was her first death case. Luckily, her consular training had included a visit to the morgue in Washington, DC. They had even viewed a dead body, for those who had never seen one. As was told to them by their instructors, best to get it over with now rather than face it for the first time in Albania or some other farflung land.

From Tess's apartment near Karlsplatz, it was a short streetcar ride most of the way to the hospital. She walked the rest of the way. The imposing and oddly ugly—for Vienna, at least—brown hospital building loomed before her. She went in and followed the signs to the *Leichenschauhaus*, the morgue. *Now that is a great German word,* Tess thought to herself. Corpse show house? The German language sure loved a literal translation.

There was a small reception area at the morgue, and she gave her name. After a few minutes, Dr. Rotkopf came out to meet her. As he introduced himself, she thought Dr. Redhead to herself, but his hair was black and matched with an impressive amount of facial hair.

He led her back toward the body and they made small talk along the way. Based on every crime show she'd ever watched, she assumed he would be eating a tuna fish sandwich with one hand while making inappropriately pithy comments about death. This was not the case.

"She was found deceased in her hotel room bed by the staff," he said. "There was no sign of foul play. She was eighty-two-years old and it appears the cause of death was cardiac arrest. The family has requested no autopsy be conducted."

"What is her name?"

Dr. Rotkopf checked the chart he carried. "Martha Freeman," he said, pronouncing the *th* in Martha like a hard *t*.

"Was she traveling with anyone?" Tess asked.

"No," the doctor answered. "I spoke with her niece on the phone. She said Mrs. Freeman had always dreamed of traveling to Europe and, since her husband died a few years back, finally decided to do it."

Oh jeez, Tess thought. *That's depressing.* If Dr. Rotkopf found it as sad as she did, he gave no sign. Tess assumed you must get immune to stories about death at some point and only focus on the facts. Otherwise, you could never do this job.

They came to the body lying on a cold, steel table. It was covered by a white blanket. The doctor handed Tess the woman's passport so she could use the photograph inside for identification purposes.

"You are ready?" Dr. Rotkopf asked.

She nodded and braced herself internally. *Please don't faint*, she said to herself.

He pulled back the sheet to reveal the old lady's face. Her hair was white and curled and she had a tasteful bit of blue eye shadow on. She looked peaceful, like she could be anyone's grandmother just taking a brief afternoon nap. It was not frightening, as Tess had expected.

She glanced at the passport. Definitely Martha Freeman. Tess nodded to the doctor and he covered the old woman back up.

"All right," Dr. Rotkopf said. "We will finish processing the body and work with the family when they arrive. They are supposed to fly in in a day or two."

"I'll have someone from our office call them tomorrow to see how we can assist."

Tess looked around the room and noticed two other bodies on tables, both covered.

"It looks as though you've had a busy day," she said.

"Average, actually. That one over there," he nodded his head to the far side of the room, "is another heart attack. However, that one there has kept our day a little more exciting."

"Oh yeah?" she asked, sensing that the doctor finally felt like a little gossip. "What's his story?"

"Murdered," Dr. Rotkopf said, a bit too melodramatically. "Just a university student. Quite sad really."

"Murdered?" Tess said. That was quite rare for Vienna. "What happened?"

"The police are still investigating, and I can't say much. What's interesting is someone tried to disguise it as a suicide."

"How'd they do that?" she asked, intrigued.

"Initially, we thought he had jumped from an upper window at the University of Vienna, but the examination shows he was either already dead or would have been soon. He had been stabbed, his carotid artery severed. If he wasn't already dead before he hit the ground, he would never have survived."

"And then someone pushed him out a window?"

The doctor shrugged.

"Perhaps. Or he fell, or perhaps jumped. We will hopefully know more soon. What he most likely didn't do was stab himself in the neck at a downward angle."

Dr. Rotkopf mimicked an overhand stabbing motion, down toward Tess's neck. If that was how the blade had gone in, it would be very difficult to do to yourself.

"No," Tess said. "I suppose not. At least he's not American."

The doctor frowned.

"I just mean," she said, blushing, "I'm glad I don't have to deal with that case. That is more excitement than I need."

The doctor nodded. "Yes," he said. "It was probably very exciting for him, as well."

CHAPTER ELEVEN

JAKE AND ANNA WALKED FROM his apartment and headed toward the old city center of Vienna. They crossed the Ring Road, which traced the one-time city walls and now stood as one of the most magnificent boulevards in the world. Along it stood many of the city's architectural icons: the majestic spires of Votiv Church, the grand baroque facade of the city hall, the opera house, Hofburg Palace, and many other sites dog-eared in every tourist's guidebook.

They walked with no destination, simply enjoying the beauty and embracing the comfortable silence. Anna was lost in her thoughts, no doubt over the death of Christian. Jake hoped more than anything that she didn't have anything to do with it.

As for himself, Jake was still trying to puzzle out Mira's unusual behavior. She clearly had been upset already when she arrived at the apartment, but Anna's presence and the talk of Christian's death had really set her off. Jake had never seen such a display of emotion from his Serbian roommate.

She was always the introvert of their trio. Although they had a good time together, Mira never let things get out of hand. She always stopped at two drinks. She was always in bed before eleven. Her homework was always completed, not just on time, but early. Jake imagined that Mira came from a background of poverty and want, and that she had no intention of allowing her opportunities in Vienna to go to waste.

They turned down a small, quiet street called *Rosengasse*, or Rose Lane, and maneuvered around a family of Italian tourists, maps in hand. The towering steeple of St. Stephen's Cathedral, which marked the heart of the city center, was momentarily obscured by the buildings around them.

"Are you sure you've never met Mira?" Jake asked, interrupting the silence. "Maybe you had a class together?"

"I don't think so. I would have remembered. She is very pretty." Anna sounded distracted.

Jake had to agree—it was the first thing he'd noticed when he moved into the flat. It took about five minutes with her to realize there would never be anything between them, though. Friends, for certain, but romance was just not in the cards. Jake wasn't sure that Helmut had come to the same conclusion yet.

"I just don't understand what set her off like that," Jake said. He slowed to allow Anna to quickly look in the window of a candy shop they passed.

"I don't know, Jake," she said. "I'm not sure what you want me to say."

"Well, I apologize for her. She didn't have any right to snap at you like that. Not after the day you've had."

"It's okay," Anna said. "I'm sure she had her reasons."

She seemed momentarily lost in thought, as though remembering a dream. For a moment, Jake thought she was going to cry.

"What is it?"

Anna shook her head slightly and started walking again, forcing him to quickly catch up and navigate around more tourists. She returned to her silence and the two of them walked a few minutes more before coming to *Stephansplatz*, the main square before St. Stephen's Cathedral. The square was packed with tourists and those who wanted to part them from their money.

The cathedral, or *Stephansdom* as it was known in German, loomed before them. The main tower of the cathedral, known colloquially as *Steffl* by the locals, soared more than 450-feet high, and was a major landmark of the city. The cathedral, in one form or another, had been here for more than eight hundred years and had witnessed countless memorable moments in history, from the funerals of Mozart and Vivaldi, to Nazi and Russian troops fighting in the streets of Vienna in April of 1945.

Jake was a bit embarrassed to admit that he had lived in Vienna for a few months now and had yet to enter the cathedral. He was a big history buff and loved to look at the exterior, but he wasn't religious and his general intolerance of tourist crowds often kept him away from the magnificent building.

"Do you see this line marked on the stones here?" Anna asked, pointing toward the ground in front of the church. It was partially obscured by passersby, but it appeared to be the outline of a small building. Dozens of tourists walked right over it, oblivious to its presence, just as Jake had done countless times.

"What is it?"

"It marks the location of another chapel that is beneath our feet. It is thought to be as old as *Stephansdom*, but was forgotten for hundreds of years and only rediscovered in the 1970s." Jake and Anna looked at the ground while the crowds flowed around them. "Follow me. I'll show you."

Anna led them down into the U-Bahn stop for *Stephansdom*, but instead of heading toward the train platform, they turned down a narrow corridor partially hidden by construction. In a dimly lit corner, just a few dozen feet away from the bustling foot traffic of the metro station, stood a large glass wall that looked down on the foundation of the ancient chapel marked above. Jake felt as though he'd just stepped into a Dan Brown novel.

It was dimly lit and wooden walkways had been built to allow the preservation work to continue. It was remarkably well preserved, bits of fresco still visible along the edge of the ceiling. In the far end of the chapel, behind where the altar would typically be, was a round hole that appeared to be a well.

A large sign to the side called it the Virgil Chapel, after a noble family that took ownership of it later in its history. Its true origin was still uncertain.

"That's crazy," he said. "I never would have known."

"Most people don't. They're building a little museum here now—soon it will be as busy as every other tourist site, but I like it now. It feels like a secret."

Jake agreed. A few others came into the tunnel while they stood, but for the most part it was quiet. It gave them the chance to appreciate the chapel, and think back on a life from hundreds of years earlier. They stood quietly a few minutes.

"Why do you think Christian jumped?" he finally asked.

"I don't know," Anna said after a moment. He turned to look at her, but she wouldn't meet his gaze. "He was upset about our relationship. We never truly know why anyone does what they do, do we? Particularly not in those final moments."

He thought about Lucy and knew Anna was right. He had been close to his sister when they were younger. Sure, he was five years older and she had endured his my-sister-is-a-total-pest phase, but they'd come out strong on the other side. He had loved Lucy very much. He hoped she'd known that.

They walked in silence for a few moments. Jake wondered whether to confront Anna about the fact that he'd seen her at the window.

"I believe he was seeing someone else," Anna said. "That is why I ended the relationship."

"Why do you think that?"

"He was acting very distracted. Very…how do you say it? Sneaky? He denied it, but I am not stupid." Her voice hardened, and she finally looked at him. "I know what was happening." It felt as though she was challenging Jake to deny it.

If that was true, he thought, she was right that Christian probably wouldn't have committed suicide. Someone starting a new relationship wouldn't do that, even if they were upset about ending an older one.

"Why would Christian have been in Professor Schmidt's office?" Jake asked. "Did he have classes with Schmidt?"

Anna shook her head, but didn't say anything.

"It doesn't make any sense," Jake continued.

"I know that you saw me," she said quietly.

He looked to her. "I did. Why didn't you answer me when I called out?"

"Whatever you think happened, it isn't what you think."

"I don't know what to think, Anna."

"Maybe he was looking for me, the same as you. I came to the office to talk to Herr Professor Schmidt."

"Was he there? Professor Schmidt, I mean? If so, he would have had to have been in the room when Christian died."

Jake had taken an instant dislike to the professor, and he thought the feeling was probably mutual. For both of them, Anna was the reason. Jake found it hard to imagine the older, scholarly man pushing Christian from his office window, but it didn't seem a stretch for the two of them to have been fighting over Anna.

"The professor was not there when I got there. No one was. The door was cracked open, so I looked inside and found the window open and a few things knocked from the desk. I think someone had been fighting."

"But if that's true, then it doesn't sound like Christian jumped."

"Maybe he fell," Anna said. "I don't know."

"Or maybe he was pushed." Obviously they were both thinking it. It was Schmidt's office. Who else could it have been?

"That's when you looked out the window and I saw you?" Jake pressed.

She nodded. "Even so far below and with his body like that, I didn't want to believe it was Christian. I didn't want him to be dead." Her voice broke, and she took a few sharp breaths.

Jake awkwardly put his arm around her shoulders. She turned and buried her face in his chest.

"It's okay, Anna," he said, talking into her blonde hair. "We'll figure it out. We will find out what happened to Christian."

He wanted to comfort her, but as he looked down on the shadowy crypt through the glass, part of him wondered if he really wanted to know the truth.

CHAPTER TWELVE

JAKE WALKED ANNA HOME IN the cool Vienna night. He found that she lived not very far from him, in an apartment complex for students in the eighth district. He left her at the front door of her building, their parting a simple hug that felt more like a brother comforting a sister than any chance at future romance.

As he walked home, he thought how different the city felt after dark. Bright lights illuminated the major sights with a golden glow, but countless alleys and side streets promised mysteries, and the buildings were decorated with statues and busts that had taken on a sinister air now that the sun was down.

The statues had been one of the first things to make an impression on him in the city. It was amazing to him how dark and downright evil many of the faces appeared. Although there was the occasional cherub or heroic figure, many more had a slightly demonic appearance that was further reinforced by the weather of time. He did his best to ignore them as he walked quickly home.

Along the way, he stopped at a Turkish food stand and grabbed a falafel sandwich, the fried chunks of chick pea probably the last thing his stomach needed, but he realized he hadn't eaten much today.

Jake looked forward to tomorrow being Saturday and having a chance to rest. He had told Anna that he would call her, but couldn't tell if she wanted that or not. He found her extraordinarily difficult to read, which made him question just how good a psychologist he would actually be.

As he walked, he thought about his studies. Did he ever have any real intention of becoming a psychologist? Jake didn't even know if that was what he wanted. The few classes he had taken back in the States had been interesting enough that when he was finally forced to choose a major it seemed to make sense. When he'd decided he needed to study abroad, Vienna was the logical fit, with its ties to Sigmund Freud and the presence of a psychologist's or psychiatrist's office on nearly every block.

If he was honest with himself, though, the truth was he didn't care what he studied. He didn't even really care where he was, as long as it wasn't back in his hometown in Ohio. There was nothing for him there but bad memories that he wanted to avoid.

Jake opened the door of his apartment quietly, in case the others were asleep. It was dark inside except for one light that had been left on in the kitchen, probably from Helmut. Jake locked the door behind him and went into the kitchen for a glass of water to wash down the dry sandwich he'd eaten on the way.

"Jake?" he heard Mira say. She stood in the doorway, darkness behind her. She was in her pajamas, but still managed to look more put together than she had earlier—as though she must have gotten at least a little sleep.

He looked up, but returned to drinking his water without acknowledging her, still pissed at the way she'd behaved earlier. He was used to Mira's stormy moods, but Anna was a good person who had just lost someone important to her. Mira had no right to snap at her.

"I'm sorry for earlier," she said, her voice husky. "I should not have yelled. It was not appropriate."

"No," Jake said. "It wasn't."

"I know. I was upset."

"Why, Mira? That's all we wanted to know. We are your friends. What happened to you today?"

"I can't talk about it right now," Mira said quietly. "I just wanted to apologize. To your friend, as well."

Jake didn't want to hear it. If she wasn't willing to tell him what was going on, he didn't have time for apologies. He and Helmut did a lot to endure her often unpredictable moods, but with everything that had transpired in the last twenty-four hours, he didn't need to add Mira's drama to his life.

"Whatever," he said. "I'm going to bed."

"Jake," she called after him, but he went into his room and shut the door.

He heard her stop outside his door, and could see the shadow of her feet in the crack. Jake pictured Mira with her fist next to the door, deciding whether to knock. Nothing came, and after a few seconds she left.

Jake stripped down to his boxers and got into bed with his laptop. He needed sleep, but decided to first check the internet. He rarely had email of any importance and Facebook often made him feel more alone than anything, but it was a habit that was hard to break.

The first story in his feed was a photograph of Jessica Nguyen. She stood next to a brand new, midnight blue Honda Civic. The smile plastered on her face was so large it was impossible for Jake not to smile back. "My first car!!" it read in the caption. It already had ninety-seven "likes," and Jake added his own.

God, Jake thought. *Sarah driving*. She and Lucy had been inseparable as kids. It was hard to think of his kid sister ever being old enough to drive. It was even harder to know that she would never have the chance.

It had all been so much easier before Lucy died. They'd been a more-or-less normal family. It wasn't all hugs and rainbows, but they got along—occasionally even did a family evening out. All in all, their family was more like a comfortable friendship. Yes, they loved each other, but there was no reason to bring it up. It was just a given.

He was never quite certain what upset the equilibrium. Jake had gone to college. For a while he blamed himself for everything that had transpired, as though somehow his absence was too much for the family to manage. It didn't seem egotistical at the time, but looking back he realized how self-centered he'd been.

With everything else—life, you could say—in the way, no one in the family had really paid attention to Jake's sister and her changing life. Lucy had been struggling in high school—not academically, but socially. Jake's mom didn't understand how that could be.

Lucy was friendly and pretty. She always had friends, but looking back Jake could tell that the group she hung with in high school were outsiders. The kids that most moms and dads warned you about, but somehow Jake's parents had failed to see it. Lucy dyed her blonde hair raven-black and started wearing makeup that drove Mom crazy.

It would be two years since Lucy's death soon, and everything was a mess, though his parents tried to hide that fact. Jake felt guilty. It was as though his mother felt she needed to be strong for him. After her initial mourning, she had worked hard to bring life back to normal, but a dropped glass can never be fully repaired. Jake had left. Not only home, but the entire country to get away from the past. His father had retreated into his work, no longer interested in anything.

It didn't take Sigmund Freud to understand Jake was projecting too much of Lucy's death into the situation with Anna. Did he really believe helping out Anna—someone he barely knew-would make up for the pain he had already lived through?

He took a breath. *No*, Jake thought. *It's not the same.* Nothing would bring Lucy back. Life would never be the same in his house, but that didn't mean it was wrong to help Anna. Anyone would do the same.

CHAPTER THIRTEEN

THE UNFAMILIAR RING OF THE duty phone woke Tess from a restless sleep. For a moment, she continued to lie in bed and stare at the damned thing. A large part of her sleep-addled brain wanted to ignore it, but she knew it would do no good. It wasn't as though the Marine at Post One would give up. If he couldn't reach her, he'd keep calling people until someone answered, and it would all come back on her head in the end.

"U.S. Embassy duty officer," she answered, trying to sound alert.

"Yes, ma'am. This is the Marine at Post One. I have a call from a woman in the States who would like to speak to someone about her son. She says he is missing."

Tess sighed. "Thanks. Put her through."

The Marine patched the woman through, told her she was on the line with an embassy officer, and then he dropped from the call. There was just the slightest delay in the international call, enough to make conversation even more awkward than it already was.

"Hello, this is Tess McIntosh. I work at the embassy here in Austria. What can I do for you?

For a moment there was silence on the other end, and Tess thought the connection had been lost. She started to repeat herself when the woman spoke. It took them a moment to get synched up to the delay.

"I'm sorry to call so late," the woman said. "Or early, I guess? It's late here. I forget the time difference. What time is it there?"

"That's fine, ma'am. It's..." Tess looked at her clock and tried not to audibly groan. "It's 5:15 a.m. here."

"Oh, well okay. It's late here." The woman seemed mollified that it was a completely appropriate time in Vienna to be taking work calls on a Saturday morning.

"What can I do for you?" Tess asked.

"Maybe I'm just being silly..."

The woman drifted off. This call was going to take forever at this rate, and all Tess wanted to do was go back to sleep. She could feel her temper rising a bit. Tess considered herself a pretty easygoing person, but if anything could push her over the edge, it was lack of sleep.

"It's fine. It's what I'm here for. Why don't you tell me what is going on. The Marine mentioned something about your son?"

"Marine?" the woman said. "Was that who answered? Does he work there too?"

"Yes," Tess said, a bit sharper than she meant. "He does. What did you tell him about your son?"

"It's probably silly, but I'm afraid my son may be in trouble. He's a student at the University of Sydney and I haven't heard from him in almost two months. I was hoping you could check on him. It's not like him not to call home for so long."

"Well, I'm sure he's okay, ma'am. Maybe he just..."

"Miss?" the woman said. "Are you still there?"

"I'm sorry. Where did you say your son is studying?"

"He's studying marine biology at the University of Sydney. It's a one-year exchange program. I know I shouldn't worry. He tells me it is a safe country, but I just—"

"Sydney, Australia?" Tess asked, trying hard not to groan.

"Yes." Doubt crept into the woman's voice. After a moment, made even more noticeable by the lag in the phone call, she spoke again. "I've called the wrong embassy, haven't I?"

"I'm afraid so, ma'am. This is the U.S. Embassy in Vienna, *Austria.* I think you're after our consulate in *Australia.*"

"I feel so stupid. I don't know how many times my son has corrected me about this."

"It's okay," Tess said. "It happens all the time." *Not really*, she thought, *but why make the woman feel dumber than she no doubt already does?*

First Jake Meyer's mom calling to check up on him, and now a wrong number from another panicked parent. Tess started to feel jealous her own mom wasn't calling to check up on her more often.

"I'm really sorry to have bothered you." The woman sighed loudly. "I feel so stupid," she said again.

"Really," Tess said. "It's no problem at all. I'm sure your son is okay. Just call the main number again and they'll transfer you to the right place. Just ask for Sydney this time."

"You're too sweet. Thank you for your understanding."

Tess looked at her clock again. 5:24 a.m. Sleep beckoned, but she found herself thinking about her call with Jake Meyer. Had he called his mother like he'd promised? She wondered what the family drama was he had hinted at.

Tess, she told herself, *are you so bored that you need stranger's problems as well as your own?*

She made a quick note in the duty officer log book about the call, and thought it would at least make for a funny office story on Monday.

As Tess drifted off to sleep, she thought she might follow up with Jake Meyer. It was only right to make sure he called home like he had promised, wasn't it?

The last thing she remembered was flipping her alarm clock on its face so as to not be reminded of the early hour. She collapsed into her comfortable blankets and was asleep minutes later.

CHAPTER FOURTEEN

JAKE WOKE ON A CHILLY Saturday morning to the sound of his front door buzzing. After pulling on last night's blue jeans and a well-worn t-shirt from the Police 2006 reunion tour, he stumbled from his room. Across the hall, Helmut came from his own bedroom in a similar state of disturbed slumber. They locked crusty eyes and came to a mutual agreement that talking was not necessary so early in the morning.

The door to Mira's room was closed, and no sound came from within. She was either still asleep or she had left the apartment early—probably the latter, knowing her schedule.

Jake answered the door while Helmut headed to the kitchen to start a pot of coffee. Next to the door of the apartment was a phone and video monitor that allowed them to see who stood at the front of the building. The image was black-and-white and small, but it was clearly two people in uniform. Jake thought they looked like the police.

He pushed the intercom button first and picked up the phone's handset.

"Yes?"

"*Polizei!*" barked one of the two. Perhaps it was his normal tone of voice, but the combination of early morning and too many WWII movies made his German sound harsh and threatening in Jake's ears.

Jake pushed the key icon on the phone, unlocking the front door of the building. The two officers entered before the screen went black. They would be upstairs in a minute.

Helmut poked his head from the kitchen. The gurgling of the coffee maker could be heard in the background.

"Did I hear the police are here?" he asked. "That doesn't seem like a good start to the day."

Jake shook the remnants of sleep from his head. No, it didn't seem good, but he didn't know what they could want. Had his parents now resorted to having the local police check on his welfare? Was it about Christian's death? Perhaps Herr Professor Rudolph Schmidt hadn't liked him stopping by the office. Was everything okay with Mira?

All of this went through his mind in a moment as he stood there facing Helmut.

"Can you go see if Mira's here?" Jake asked.

For a moment a look of concern crossed Helmut's face, but he quickly hid it with his trademark grin.

"You think she moved out and called the police on us?" He joked, but Jake also noticed how fast he moved to Mira's door. As he started to tap on the door gently and call her name, there was a knock at the front apartment door.

Jake confirmed it was the police through the peephole, slid the deadbolt, and opened the door. Before him were two Austrian police officers. One was a young woman, probably not much older than Jake—likely mid-twenties, and strikingly attractive, though the stern look on her face suggested a misplaced hand would result in a broken wrist. The other was a man, clearly the senior both in age and rank. Jake didn't know anything about Austrian police uniforms, but he knew more stripes and stars and doodads indicated seniority the world over. The man had a tiny handlebar mustache that he regularly twirled.

"Good morning," the male officer said in English. "My name is Inspector Renner and this is my colleague, Deputy Inspector Kurz. We are looking for…"

He pulled a small notepad from his chest pocket to confirm the name.

"Herr Jacob Meyer," he finished, turning the "J" sound into a "Y," as commonly happened when German speakers pronounced his name.

"I'm Jake," he said. "Can I help you?"

"Do you mind if we step inside? We have a few questions for you."

Jake stepped aside to let them pass. "Please come in."

After they were inside, he led them toward the dining room table, which was messier than he would have liked. He slid a few books down to the far end so that the chairs were free.

"Have a seat. Would you like some coffee?"

It looked as though the female officer was about to accept, but at a look from her counterpart they both declined.

Helmut stood at the edge of the room, hovering with no attempt at disguising his curiosity. Jake assumed that meant Mira was out.

"This is my roommate, Helmut," Jake explained. "Do we need privacy? He is more than happy to leave."

That only made Helmut smile bigger.

"No," said Officer Renner. "That is fine. This should not take very long."

Helmut walked past them into the kitchen to get his coffee. The two police officers and Jake sat at the table. He waited, already forming answers to dozens of hypothetical questions in his mind.

"A student died last Tuesday," Renner said. "His name was Christian Franck."

So that was why they were here. Jake set aside the hypothetical questions and tried to remain calm. He nodded.

"Christian? Yes, I know."

"Did you know Mr. Franck?" Renner asked. He had his notepad out, but hadn't written anything. Officer Kurz was taking notes, however, without looking up.

"Not really. I met him a few days prior to that, but it was just an introduction really."

"Who introduced you to him?"

Jake paused a bit too long. Officer Kurz looked up from her note taking.

"Anna Duerning," he said.

Renner nodded, as though this was expected. "And how do you know Miss Duerning?"

"We met at a café around a week ago. Since then, I've seen her around campus a few times."

"Do you know how Miss Duerning knew Mr. Franck?" Renner continued, Kurz back to her note taking.

"I believe they used to be in a relationship."

"A romantic relationship, you mean?"

"Yes," Jake said. "That is correct."

"But it was no longer?"

"The relationship?" Jake asked. "I don't think so."

Jake's gut was doing gymnastics. He tried to look over the edge of the deputy inspector's notebook to see what she was writing, but it was impossible. "Look, have you spoken to her about this? I don't know why you're asking me about someone else's love life."

Kurz gave Jake a look that froze him in his tracks, and then continued her note taking.

"We have already spoken to Miss Duerning," Renner said. "That is why we are here speaking to you."

Jake saw Helmut raise a questioning eyebrow. The police officers had their backs to him and didn't notice. Jake tried to ignore him.

"What do you mean?" Jake asked.

"Where were you at the time of Christian Franck's death?" Renner asked. Kurz looked up at Jake, awaiting his answer.

Jake's heart raced. He didn't like where this conversation had suddenly turned. Renner's gaze looked harder now, accusatory.

"I'm…I'm not sure," he finished weakly.

"It was last Tuesday at approximately eleven-thirty in the morning," Renner said.

"I think I had grabbed some lunch from a sausage stand," Jake said. "I don't really remember exactly."

"And were you alone?" Renner asked.

Jake hoped he looked calmer on the outside then he felt on the inside. His breath quickened and his stomach clenched. Why were they asking him these questions? What had Anna told them, and why hadn't she called Jake to tell him she had spoken with the police? Were they investigating him for Christian's death? It was ridiculous. Surreal.

"No," Jake said suddenly. He didn't know where it came from.

"You were not alone?" Renner clarified.

Jake could see Helmut shaking his head back and forth, mouthing the word, "No."

"No, I was not alone. I was with Anna. We had grabbed lunch together."

Both officers looked at him for a moment, and then at each other. Deputy Inspector Kurz wrote some more. This time, even Renner jotted down a note. Jake tried to read it, but between the scribbled handwriting and German language, he couldn't decipher a single word.

"And how long were you and Miss Duerning together last Tuesday?"

"I don't really remember. We grabbed lunch and walked for a bit. I know we split up that afternoon, but she came by later. Right, Helmut?"

The two officers turned to follow Jake's gaze toward Helmut. He blanched and took a sip of coffee from his mug, a highly inappropriate cartoon pig in a police uniform emblazoned on the front. Jake hoped they wouldn't notice.

"Yes," Helmut said. "Anna came by last Tuesday. Excuse me." He turned and went into the kitchen.

Before they could follow up with more questions, Jake cut in.

"Why all the questions, Officer? Christian jumped from a window."

"Mr. Franck did not commit…" Renner paused for a moment and muttered "*selbstmord*" to Kurz in German.

"Suicide," she said, the first word she had spoken.

"*Suicide*," Renner repeated. "He was murdered."

Jake felt like he might throw up.

"He was pushed from the window?" he asked.

"Possibly," Renner said. "After someone stabbed him."

Jake paled. He didn't know what to say. Part of him had always thought the suicide was unlikely. Anna had said so herself. Now the question was, who would want to kill Christian, and why?

Officer Renner stood suddenly, even catching his companion off guard. She quickly put her notepad back in her chest pocket and got up as well.

"Well, we appreciate your time, Herr Meyer," Renner said, offering his hand. "We may have some more questions in the future, but that will do for now."

"No problem at all," Jake said. "I hope you figure out who killed Christian."

"We will. Have no worries. The first step is to check alibis, so we appreciate you speaking to us this morning."

It took Jake a moment to understand what Renner had said. They had to check alibis. Anna had already told them she was with Jake? Why had she lied to them? An even better question: why had *he* lied to them? *That was idiotic.*

The officers left him a business card. As he closed the door behind them, the enormity of his deception sank in.

He turned from the door to find Helmut standing there, an uncharacteristically serious look on his face.

What the hell had he done?

CHAPTER FIFTEEN

FROM THE LIVING ROOM WINDOW, Jake could see the police detectives on the sidewalk below. They stood next to their car and had pulled packs of cigarettes from their pockets. They smoked and talked and looked up toward his window. Jake pulled back instinctively, though he thought it unlikely they could see him.

"That was very stupid, my friend Jake," said Helmut as he followed him into the room, still holding his ridiculous coffee mug.

"Yeah," Jake said. "I'm aware. What was I supposed to say, Helmut?"

"I don't know. The truth?"

Jake didn't make eye contact with his roommate as he went and collapsed on the sofa, trying to sort out what he should do. He had to find Anna and talk to her. He tried not to think *and make sure our stories line up*, since that sounded very much like something a guilty person would say.

"I believe you were, in fact, not with Anna when her boyfriend suddenly decided to fly from the window, correct?"

Jake looked up at Helmut.

"Not only flew from the window," Helmut continued, "but apparently managed to get himself stabbed first."

"Yeah," Jake said. "Apparently."

"This is no good for you."

Jake leaned back on the sofa and covered his face with his hands. He should run downstairs immediately and recant his story. He wasn't with Anna until later in the day; he didn't know where she'd been at the time of Christian's death, though he was fairly certain he saw her poke her head out the window from which her ex had taken his swan dive. He barely even knew this girl. Why was he ruining his life for her?

"No good at all," Helmut said.

"I know, Helmut!" Jake finally snapped. "I know it was a stupid thing to do—I don't know why I did it."

"Just as long as we're all on the same page here."

"I need to go see Anna," Jake said.

"Are you sure that is a good idea? They may be waiting for that."

Jake hadn't thought about that. It was possible, but he was her friend. Wouldn't it be normal for him to go comfort her during this difficult time? And what could they really do about it? It wasn't illegal for him to go there, and it wasn't like they would have bugged her apartment. Would they?

"I have to take the chance. I need to talk to her and find out what exactly happened that day. If I decide she's guilty in any way, I'll go to the police and tell them."

Helmut raised an eyebrow and took a sip of his coffee, but said nothing.

"Honestly," Jake said.

"Mm hmm," Helmut said.

~

Jake opened the door to the front of the building a crack and peeked outside. The morning sun was strong, but the police were nowhere to be seen. He noticed a few pedestrians watching him carefully, though, and realized he was making himself seem far more suspicious with his skulking. He opened the door and went out.

It was about a fifteen-minute walk or a very quick ride on the streetcar. He decided he could use the few extra minutes to clear his head and think.

He walked down Alser Strasse, passing various buildings belonging to the University of Vienna—including the large Altes AKH or "Old Hospital." It was a warren of courtyards and interconnected buildings that, true to its name, had served as the city's primary hospital for many years before eventually becoming a part of the school. Many of Jake's classes were held there, and it was a common gathering place not only for the students of the university, but also other area residents and even a few tourists who managed to escape the well-trod paths of the first district.

Anna's apartment was on a quiet street named Albert Gasse. There were a few people about, including two children riding bicycles around the plaza where her street intersected with Breitenfeld Gasse.

He found "Duerning" on the door's buzzer and pressed the button. He waited, but nothing happened. He held the button down longer. Still there was nothing. He was holding it continuously a third time when he heard her voice shout down.

"Please, Jake!"

He looked around and then up and saw her head sticking out a third-floor window. It occurred to him this was becoming a bit of a routine with them.

"Anna," Jake yelled. "I need to talk to you."

Even from twenty-five feet below, he could tell she had been crying. She also looked as though she hadn't slept in a few days.

"Come back later," Anna said. "I am very busy right now."

"I need to talk to you now, Anna," Jake said. "I'm not going to go away."

On a floor between them, an old woman stuck her head out and scowled at him. She said something in rapid German that he couldn't understand, but it didn't sound complimentary. Jake ignored her and returned to Anna.

"The police were at my house this morning," he said.

The old woman said something else and then pulled her head back inside.

"Please be quiet, Jake," Anna said, looking nervous. "Fine. Come inside."

Anna disappeared. For a moment, he thought she was going to leave him standing on the street. He determined he would not give up; he would break his way in if it came to that. However, a few seconds later there was a click from the front door and he pushed it open.

Jake bypassed the small, rickety-looking elevator and took the stairs two at a time to Anna's floor. He found her door and before he could knock, she opened it and stood before him.

His impression from outside had been spot-on. She looked tired and a little disheveled. The angelic blonde hair was tangled and the slightest blush of blue under her eyes showed her lack of sleep. She wore blue jeans and an unadorned lavender t-shirt. The bandages on her wrists appeared to have been changed again, the white gauze not much larger than a tennis player's wristband now. He wondered how badly she had actually cut herself.

Jake entered the apartment without being invited, but she stood to the side to allow him access.

Her apartment was very small and immaculately kept except for her bed, which was unmade. It was a studio-style flat and he could see just about all of it as soon as he entered, with the exception of the bathroom and a portion of the small kitchen nook. She had a newer iMac computer with an almost comically large monitor, and on the wall behind it were cork bulletin boards covered with notes and charts, most of which looked well beyond what Jake was capable of understanding.

Anna stood facing him. She looked sad and frightened. Her hands rubbed together as though washing off an invisible stain.

"The police came to my apartment this morning," Jake said.

Anna nodded. "What did you tell them?" she asked quietly.

"I lied to them, Anna," Jake said. "I don't even know why I did it. It was a stupid thing to do, and you had better convince me there was a good reason or I'll tell them the truth."

Jake was angry. The ramifications of his deception to the police were beginning to weigh on him. He didn't know much about the Austrian legal system—in fact, he didn't know too much about the American system—but he'd seen enough television and movies to know lying to the police in a criminal investigation was at best obstruction and, at worst, could be viewed as collusion.

"I'm sorry," she said. She sat on the small sofa and indicated for him to sit as well. "I could tell they thought I killed Christian."

He sat next to her, his anger beginning to subside, but not his fear.

"What did you tell them, exactly?"

"They came to talk to me about Christian. They knew we had dated. I'm sure someone else had told them about that. At first they asked about where I was during his death, and I told them I was not there. I was so scared, Jake."

"But you *were* there, Anna," Jake said. "I saw you in the window. Others probably saw you as well. They probably saw me. The police aren't going to buy my story at all."

"It isn't what they think," she said. "Do you honestly think they'll believe the suicidal ex-girlfriend didn't have anything to do with it?" She held up her bandaged wrists.

Jake didn't know what to say. Part of him had been happy that she'd never raised the story. "What happened? Why would you do something like that?"

Anna looked to her wrists and shook her head. "I wish I knew, Jake. I was just so…tired. Honestly, that was it. I was sad and angry at what was happening between Christian and me, but mostly I was just tired."

"Tired of what?"

Anna shrugged. "I don't know. Everything. School. Christian. I just didn't know what to do."

For a moment they sat in silence. Jake thought about Lucy and how terrible her final moments must have been. Had she been frightened? Sad? Or, like Anna, had she simply had enough?

After a few seconds, Anna spoke. "It looks worse than it is. The doctors actually told me there was no way I would have died from my cuts. I felt so stupid afterward."

"There is no reason to feel stupid. We've all been through tough times."

"Did you ever try to kill yourself with an old kitchen knife?"

Jake laughed. "No, I can't say that I have." The gravity of the situation returned to him, and he became serious once more. "The police told me Christian was stabbed first. Then he was either pushed or fell from the window."

Anna sniffed, tears pooling in her eyes. "Yes," she said. "They told me, as well."

"You must have been in the office just minutes after it happened, though," Jake said. "You didn't see anyone?"

"No," she said. "You've been up there. It is a maze of hallways and rooms. Someone easily could have left before I got there without me seeing them. There are multiple stairwells as well as elevators. I never found Herr Professor Schmidt."

She was right: the building was confusing, and there were always people in the halls, but it still didn't feel right to Jake. The coincidence seemed too strong, but what was the alternative? That Anna stabbed Christian? He couldn't believe she was capable of that. *That's what Mom keeps saying about Lucy.* He shook the thought away.

"Why didn't you tell the police this?"

"I could tell they didn't believe I wasn't involved. They saw this," she held up her bandaged wrists. "And they came to their own conclusions.

"The police," she continued disdainfully, her brow furrowed. "Particularly that woman. The one taking all of the notes. I could tell she was judging me. She wanted me to be guilty."

"So what did you tell them?"

"I told them I was studying with a friend at a café. I said I was with you."

Anna looked at him, tears in her eyes. As hurt and frightened as she appeared, part of Jake felt he was being manipulated.

"What did you tell the police?" Anna asked quietly.

"I said I was with you and that we'd had lunch. They acted as though they bought my story, but it really isn't the same as yours. I think they knew I was lying."

"I'm sure it is okay, Jake. It will be all right."

"Christian was stabbed, Anna," Jake said. "Who would do that? What happened in that office?"

"I don't even understand why he would be in Herr Professor Schmidt's office. He doesn't have any classes with him. He had no reason to be there. He has no connection at all to the professor."

"He did have one very good connection to him, Anna. He had you."

CHAPTER SIXTEEN

TESS MANAGED TO DRAG HERSELF to the shower a few hours after hanging up with her early-morning caller. She was exhausted. She never slept well when she was on call as duty officer. Although middle-of-the-night calls were fairly rare in Vienna, the fact that they could happen interfered with her ability to check out and go to sleep.

She leaned against the cool tiles in the shower and let the hot water pour down her back. The steam soothed her and began to awaken her senses.

Vienna was beautiful. Most of her colleagues had been incredibly jealous-though supportive-when her name was called for the assignment. They had been excited about their own postings, from Jakarta to Port-au-Prince.

Still, it was hard not to feel down at times, even surrounded by such opportunity and with work she generally enjoyed. She didn't really have any friends outside of work and even within the embassy community, it was more close acquaintances than anything else. She was still in touch with a few friends back in Massachusetts, but there was increasingly little they had in common.

"Perspective, Tess," she said to herself. It was her mantra. Things could always be worse.

After dressing and applying just a touch of makeup, she was ready for the day. Though it wasn't her job, she had already decided she would go check on Jake Meyer personally. The call from the distraught mother in the middle of the night had gotten her thinking about the American once more.

It was her curiosity and, she had to admit, a touch of loneliness that urged her toward tracking him down. As she spent most of her time on the visa line interviewing holiday seekers, Tess didn't have much of an opportunity to work on American citizen cases. For once, Thurston had given her something other than those boring visa cases, and she was determined to do it right.

Tess convinced herself she was just going the extra mile. What if Jake Meyer really was in trouble? It was the least she could do. She decided to go out, grab a coffee, and swing by.

Her position didn't come with a lot of actual power, but there was the impression that it did.

"My name is Tess McIntosh," she thought to herself. "I'm from the American Embassy."

It had a great ring to it. She'd been disappointed to find that some of her more veteran colleagues were a bit jaded about the career, but to her it was all still very exciting.

It was a beautiful sunny day as she left her apartment building. The neo-Gothic central spire of the city hall loomed over the pretty plaza in front. She cut through the little park and stopped at a local café where she ordered coffee to go, something that Americans from a Starbucks world craved but wasn't always easy to find in the café culture of Austria.

She walked down busy streets, the ornate buildings of the University of Vienna lining her way. Between the traffic, the tourists, the bicyclists, and the streetcars, walking in the city required her full attention, but she didn't mind. She loved the bustle and the sense of life the city had, even with thousands of years of history behind it.

She found the address, double checking it against the paper in her hand. A list of buttons with occupant names stood next to the door. There weren't actually any names listed beside Jake's apartment number, it just said *Studenten*. Students. She imagined it must be a university-owned building with a high-enough turnover that it wasn't worth their time to change out the name plate.

She pushed the button and waited. After a moment, a man's voice answered in German. As part of her training for the assignment, Tess had been given nearly eight months of German lessons from the famous Foreign Service Institute outside of Washington, DC.

"Hello, my name is Tess McIntosh," she replied in German. "I'm from the American Embassy. Does Jake Meyer live here?"

"Jake?" the voice said, and switched to English. "Yes, but he is not home."

"Do you know when he might be back?"

The man on the other end of the intercom laughed.

"He is having a very busy day today. Are you with the police?"

That caught her off guard. It couldn't possibly be considered a good sign.

"No," she said. "Are the police looking for him?"

"You should talk to him yourself. If you have something to write with, I can give you his handy number."

In German, the word for a cell phone is "handy." It never stopped being funny to Tess.

"No," she said. "I have it. I will give him a call. Thank you."

"Tell him Helmut said to not be so stupid."

"Um, you got it."

Tess stepped away from the door and out of sight of the camera and pulled out her cell phone. She had the piece of paper in the other hand and was typing in Jake's number when her phone rang. Looking at the number, she realized it was the same.

"Tess McIntosh," she said.

"Ms. McIntosh," a man's voice said. "I don't know if you remember me, but we spoke the other day on the phone. You called to check on me after my mom called the embassy. My name is Jake Meyer."

"Yes," she said. "I remember. Actually, I wanted to speak to you."

"You did?" he said. "What for?"

She suddenly felt very self-conscious about tracking him down. "To close out my case. I just needed to make sure you had contacted your mother." She felt silly, like she was reprimanding a child when Jake wasn't much younger than her.

"Uh, yeah. I did call her after we spoke. I've just been really busy lately. I'm sorry she called you guys."

"No," Tess said, glad Jake wasn't here in person to see her blush. "I understand. Is everything okay back home?"

"That's a problem for another time. I was hoping we could meet. I think I'm in trouble. I don't know who else I can turn to."

He sounded frightened and suddenly young. Tess knew there was a good chance that whatever trouble he had managed to get himself into, it was not something she could help with. Yet again, she cursed the American media for leaving its citizens with the impression that they all had a free pass the moment they left U.S. borders.

"Tell me where you want to meet."

Tess knew the location as soon as he mentioned it. It was less than ten minutes away. She agreed to meet him there and hung up the phone. Maybe this wasn't such a simple case after all.

CHAPTER SEVENTEEN

JAKE ARRIVED AT SIGMUND FREUD Park and went to the quieter area off to the side of the main grassy expanse. The weather was nice and the park was full of people, mostly students relaxing. The park offered bright orange lounge chairs free for use, and these were scattered about as people enjoyed the last vestiges of the summer sun as the city slipped into autumn. A nearby group of five or six college students tossed a Frisbee, their laughter infectious. Jake envied their day.

The towering spires of Votivkirche loomed over the park, the twin peaks delicate and lacy in white sandstone. Most of the front facade of the church was covered in scaffolding as workers attempted to undo the damage of automobile exhaust never considered by the architect. Nearby stood the imposing main building of the University of Vienna, where Jake had seen Christian's mangled body on the sidewalk below and Anna in the window above. It seemed simultaneously a distant dream and a nightmare from which he had yet to awaken. Tourists walked beneath the window with no idea of the tragedy that had recently occurred.

Jake sat on a wooden bench and waited for the consular officer to arrive. He had no idea what she looked like, but he had given her a description of himself and she sounded familiar with the park. Several pigeons worked their way closer toward his feet after he sat, hoping the newcomer would be willing to toss them a few scraps of food.

He watched them in their comical herky-jerky motion, their pinpoint eyes locking with his own. Jake envied them for a moment. Nothing to think about apart from where they'd get their next meal.

Sure, you occasionally lost a friend to a surprise Rottweiler attack, but overall life was pretty easy. At least they didn't have to worry about police investigations and murder allegations.

A pretty young woman with chestnut brown hair pulled back into a ponytail approached him. She was dressed casually but with a certain flair for style, a silky gray scarf looped around her neck.

"Jake?" she asked.

He stood and offered his hand.

"You must be Miss McIntosh," he said.

"You can call me Tess. Did you want to sit here?"

"Sure," he motioned to the empty spot on the bench next to him. "Please."

She was younger than he'd expected, probably not much older than himself. He told her so.

"It's my first assignment. I joined the Foreign Service pretty much right out of college."

"I guess I never even gave any thought to who the people are that work at embassies."

"Most people don't," Tess said. "At least not until they need our help."

"Yeah," Jake said. "I guess that's true."

He was silent. He suddenly felt like a fool for calling this woman. He didn't know anything about her, and he really doubted there was anything she could do for him. He was in over his head. He had lied to the police—he could go to jail.

"So you spoke with your mother?" Tess asked at last, breaking the ice.

"Yeah," Jake said. "I'm sorry about that. I guess I look like a pretty deadbeat son. She just worries about me."

"Look, I don't want to pry, but why is she so worried about you? No offense, but you're a bit old to have your mom calling to check up on you."

"My feelings exactly. It's…well, it's complicated. My sister died recently, and since then…" Jake didn't really want to talk about it. Maybe he should, but this was neither the time nor the place.

"I'm sorry," Tess said, her face softening. "I think I understand."

"That's really not what I called you about, though." Jake shook his head, trying to shake away the bad memories, images from the news of bodies covered in white sheets being pulled from the school. No time for that now. "I have real problems. Not just an overprotective mother."

"Okay," Tess said. "I have to tell you up front though, a lot of people think the embassy can do a lot more than we really can. I can't promise I'll be able to help you."

She paused a moment, until Jake looked her in the eye. "Especially if you've done something illegal."

He nodded. "I understand, and I haven't. Done something illegal, that is."

Tess audibly let out a sigh of relief.

"Well, I mean, I have, but not really."

He noticed her instantly tense up again.

"Maybe you better start from the beginning," Tess suggested.

As they sat on the bench in the cool shade along the side of Freud Park—so-named for being a regular haunt of the world's most famous psychologist during his time living in Vienna—Jake told Tess about what had happened to him over the last week. He told her of his first encounter with Anna at the café, her public fight with Christian, all the way up to finding the body dead on the ground below the window at the nearby university building.

Tess looked over at the window, so high above the busy sidewalk below, and shuddered.

"The police told me he was already dead before he hit the ground, though," Jake said. "Or would have been soon. Somebody stabbed him, presumably in that room."

"The police told you this?" Tess asked.

Jake went on to describe the visit from the police that morning and how he had provided an alibi for Anna, though he hadn't actually been with her.

"Jake, that was really stupid," Tess cut in.

"I've been hearing that a lot today," Jake said. "I know it was a dumb thing to do. I honestly don't know what I was thinking, but I believe Anna. I don't think she would have stabbed Christian. I certainly don't think she is capable of throwing him from a window."

Jake stopped for a moment and thought. "Actually, I hadn't thought about it, but there is no way she could have thrown him through that window. Christian wasn't the biggest guy, but Anna is small. She'd never have been able to do it. Especially not a struggling victim."

"Maybe he fell from the window after the stabbing?"

Jake thought about it. "I guess he could have, but does that make any sense? I just don't know."

"Have you spoken to Anna since the police came by?" Tess asked.

He told her of going to Anna's place, and Anna's story about showing up on the scene after the fact.

"And you believe her?" Tess asked.

He thought about it for a moment. He had only met Anna for the first time less than a week ago. They had maybe spent a total of a few hours together since then. Was he willing to risk everything on his gut?

"I do," Jake said, and found he believed his words. "I went up there later that day to try and find her, and it really is a maze of corridors and rooms. She could have easily missed the real killer."

"Then who is the real killer? Why was Christian there, and who would want to kill him?"

"I have an idea," Jake said. "I've been thinking about it, and only one thing makes any sense."

"What's that?" Tess asked.

"It has to be her professor—this guy Schmidt. I get the feeling Anna is afraid of him, and he seemed to take an instant dislike to me when he saw me talking with her the other day. I think he's in love with Anna."

"How old is Schmidt?"

"He's got to be at least sixty, probably more," Jake said.

Tess curled a lip like she had just stepped in gum. "That's gross."

"Maybe so, but that doesn't mean it doesn't happen. If I'm thinking the guy has a crush on Anna and I only just met him, it would make sense that Christian came to the same conclusion. Maybe he went to confront Schmidt."

"The talk goes bad. They fight. Schmidt stabs Christian and tosses him from the window?" Tess looked skeptical. "This is your theory?"

It sounded ridiculous when she said it, but what was the alternative? Anna did it? Christian stabbed himself? Nothing else made sense, and he told Tess as much.

"It's possible," Tess said. "So when are you going to tell the police this?"

"The police?" Jake asked. "I can't go to the police. I lied to them. I need something solid to bring them or they'll end up thinking I killed Christian."

Jake noticed Tess's look change slightly, her eyes scrunching up as though suddenly lost in thought. He didn't like the look.

"Which I didn't do," he quickly added. "Honestly."

She held the look a moment longer, but then relaxed. "I believe you," she said.

"Good," Jake said. "Because it's the truth."

"I know. We actually have lie detection as part of our consular training. It helps with visa interviews."

"Seriously?" Jake asked. "So you can always tell when someone is lying to you?"

"Always," she said. "Keep that in mind."

Jake thought she was screwing with him, but couldn't be certain. He was starting to like talking to Tess. She was far from the stuffy bureaucrat he'd imagined.

"I have to tell you, Jake, I'm not sure what I can really do to help. You lied to the police. I can't keep you out of jail—in fact, I should turn you in."

"You can't!" Jake said, suddenly doubting his first impression of her.

"I won't." Tess locked her brown eyes on his. "At least not right now, but I don't think there is much I can do."

"I understand," Jake said. "I just needed someone to talk to."

It felt good to tell someone about his situation, but he was still disappointed. He wasn't sure what he had expected, but he'd thought Tess would be able to do something.

Even without help from the embassy, though, Jake felt he was on the right track. He was sure Professor Schmidt had something to do with this, but he had no proof. However, he also couldn't shake the feeling that Anna wasn't being one hundred percent honest with him. He needed more before he could go to the police.

"I'll tell you what," Tess said. "I'll do some digging on my end. No promises!"

"That would be great," Jake said, relief washing over him. "Anything you can find out will help."

"Give me until Monday night. I'll let you know what I learn."

"Maybe a drink Monday night, then?" Jake asked, sounding as casual as possible.

Tess raised an eyebrow.

"I just meant to trade info. Nothing more than that. Honest."

She eyed him for a moment, those eyes scrunching. "Okay," she said. "Monday night at seven p.m. at the Bagpiper. You know it?"

He did, and promised to meet her. He hoped she could find out something. Almost anything would be more than he had at the moment.

"See you then," Jake said, for the first time feeling the slightest glimmer of optimism after this terrible day.

CHAPTER EIGHTEEN

JAKE ENTERED HIS APARTMENT AND found Mira sitting at the dining room table, drinking tea and reading a book. Helmut was nowhere to be seen. She quickly dog-eared her page and set the book down in front of her.

"Jake," Mira said. "I need to talk to you. I need to explain."

He sighed. This was more drama that he just couldn't handle at the moment. Of everyone he knew, Mira was the one he least expected this from.

"Look," he said. "It's been a rough few days. I don't know why you were upset the other day, but it isn't a big deal. Let's just forgive and forget, all right?"

He walked into the living room and sat down. Jake was tired, but needed to come up with more information to prove his theory that Professor Schmidt was somehow involved with Christian's death.

Mira entered the room and sat next to him, much closer than was customary for the typically reserved Serbian woman. She looked at him and he saw tears in her eyes. Judging by the lines around her eyes and puffiness there, she'd been crying quite a bit lately.

"You do not understand, Jake. I need to talk to you about Christian and Anna."

"Christian and Anna? You know them?"

After the strange confrontation between Mira and Anna the other night, he had asked Anna repeatedly if she knew his roommate and she had denied it. Was Mira indicating Anna had lied to him?

"I know of Anna, but I had never met her before the other night when she was here. I had only seen pictures of her. I also saw her a few times around campus, when I followed her. She did not know me."

"You followed Anna?" Jake asked, his head spinning. "What are you talking about, Mira?"

"I had to see her. I wanted to see why Christian cared for this girl. What made her so special." As she talked, Mira's tone took on a bitter edge. There was anger there, as well as jealousy.

Jake began to understand where the story was headed.

"You did not know Anna, but you did know Christian," he prompted.

Mira nodded. "Christian and I were together for a time, but he ended it."

"When was this?" Jake asked.

"A few months back, in the spring. It only lasted for a short while."

"A few months ago? But Anna told me they had dated for nearly a year."

Mira looked down at her hands, but after a moment she met Jake's eyes, her typical fearless gaze fixed on him.

"He started it," Mira said. "We are...were in the same history class together. It started as studying and then it just...grew."

"Did Anna ever find out?" Jake asked.

"I don't know," Mira said. "I don't think he told her, but he stopped talking to me. He would avoid me during class and would not answer my calls."

Jake couldn't believe all of this drama had been going on right under his nose. The affair would have been before he arrived, but surely Mira's desperate attempts to call Christian must have still been going on after they became roommates. She spent a lot of time in her room. He had always assumed she was just studying.

They were both quiet, lost in their separate thoughts.

"Anna didn't kill Christian," Jake said.

Mira didn't respond.

"Do you believe me?" Jake asked, looking at her.

"I know you believe that," she eventually said. "But we never know what we are capable of until we are pushed too far."

"That's true," Jake said. "I guess. But Anna?"

"Maybe you are right," Mira said. "Anna is too weak for that." Before Jake could say anything, she continued. "I'm sorry, Jake. I know she is your friend, but she could never have killed Christian. She couldn't kill anyone. She couldn't even kill herself."

It was harsh, but it was true. Although he hadn't known her long, Anna struck him more as one for dramatic actions without any lasting consequences than a true believer.

"That's a pretty mean thing to say," Jake said. "But I see your point."

Mira shrugged, as if to indicate that her bluntness was not a concern.

"Why do you think Christian was in Professor Schmidt's office?" Jake asked. "Did you know that was who the office belonged to?"

"Yes, I knew," she said. "A day before his death, I saw Christian at school. For the first time in weeks, he actually acknowledged me. I thought he was ready to try again. I knew that Anna had broken it off with him."

"What did he say?"

"He said, 'I know who he is."'

"What does that mean?" Jake asked, not following. "Who was *he*?"

"I'm not positive, but I think he meant Professor Schmidt."

"'I know who he is,'" Jake repeated. "He knew Schmidt was in love with Anna?"

"In love with Anna?" Mira said. "What are you talking about? You think the professor was in love with Anna?"

"You think an old man can't fall for a young, beautiful student?"

He noticed her scowl at the word beautiful, but chose to ignore it.

"Of course it is possible," Mira said, her voice betraying her skepticism.

"It happens all the time where I'm from. I bet it happens in Serbia, too. And I'm sure it could happen here."

"You think Christian and Herr Professor Schmidt fought over Anna?" Mira asked. She thought about it, but shook her head. "I don't think so. Christian wasn't really the jealous type. He wasn't the type to fight for what he loved."

Jake thought there was more to that statement than even Mira realized.

"Perhaps Christian wasn't a fighter," Jake said. "But that doesn't mean Schmidt wouldn't fight if confronted. I don't know anything about him, but he doesn't seem like a particularly nice guy. Do you know him better than I do?"

"No," she admitted. "But I just don't see it. A professor—an older man, at that—stabbed Christian and pushed him out a window? It just doesn't sound right."

"It has to be," Jake insisted, but felt doubts gnawing at his gut. "What else could Christian be talking about?"

"Maybe," Mira said slowly. It was obvious she still wasn't buying his theory.

"You didn't get any more than that? Just, 'I know who he is'?" Jake asked.

"I tried!" she said. "I was so excited that he was finally speaking to me, but he just repeated it again and ran off. I tried calling him later that day, but he didn't answer. I thought I would catch him at our next class, but then…"

"It was too late," Jake finished.

"Yes," she said. "It was too late."

CHAPTER NINETEEN

FOR THE THIRD TIME THAT morning, Jake tried calling Anna but got no answer. He sent a short text asking her to call him as soon as she saw the message. When he'd left her apartment the day before, they had agreed to meet this morning.

Jake wanted to go into Schmidt's office, and knew she would be able to let him know his schedule so that he could slip in undetected. He didn't understand where she could be and why she wasn't answering his calls. Could the police have picked her up?

He still worried that Inspector Renner and his partner Kurz were going to show up at his apartment at any moment to arrest him for lying. It was only by sheer luck that his story somewhat supported Anna's, but he doubted they would buy it. Jake had said they had lunch at a sausage stand together while Anna said she had been studying with him in a café. They could try to spin it to make it sound like they were talking about the same thing, but he knew if he were a police officer, he'd never believe them.

Jake went to the kitchen and grabbed a bowl of cereal. He took it to the living room and sat down on the sofa to eat. Helmut sat opposite him, playing on his iPad. Mira had left early that morning and neither of them knew where she had gone. She rarely told them what she did or where she went.

"The police have kept the stabbing very quiet," Helmut said, not looking up. "There have not been any news stories since the original ones that said Christian either jumped or fell from that window."

"I'm not surprised," Jake said around a mouthful of cereal. "Violent crimes don't happen very often in Vienna, particularly something like this. Plus, it probably makes their investigation easier without all the extra attention."

"This must seem normal to you," Helmut said.

"Normal? How in the hell is this normal?"

"Coming from America, I mean. Things like this happen in the States all the time. I have seen the news."

Jake rarely felt the need to defend his homeland, but he did at least try to correct some of the largest misconceptions.

"I guess things like this happen," Jake said. "But it isn't like it is common. We're a huge country with a giant population, nearly four times that of Germany. It may seem like there is a lot of violence in the news, but that's just because the media loves to report this crap."

"What about where you come from? What is your hometown again?"

"Tulson, Ohio," Jake said after a second. "Yeah, we've had our problems, too."

He thought of Lucy. He could tell that Helmut was about to ask more questions, and jumped in before he could start.

"I've been trying to reach Anna all morning and she isn't answering the phone."

"You should give her up, Jake," Helmut said. "She isn't that pretty."

Jake had updated Helmut on everything that had happened, except the details Mira had told him. Helmut thought he hid it quite well, but Jake could tell he was interested in their roommate. Mira probably knew, as well. Jake didn't want to dash what little hope Helmut had by explaining she had been seeing Christian and later obsessing over him for months.

"It isn't how she looks, Helmut. I don't think she did it. I believe her."

"If you say so," Helmut said. "If she had a giant wart on her face and buck teeth, you might not feel so compelled to save her."

"She couldn't have done it," Jake insisted. "Plus, she reminds me of my little sister."

The words were out of his mouth before he really had time to process them, as though he were thinking out loud. Like that, the reality hit him: that was why he was so drawn to her. Anna was beautiful, but he knew he wasn't romantically attracted to her.

He wanted to protect her. She seemed so vulnerable. Physically she appeared like a beam of moonlight, blonde-haired and blue-eyed, but inside she was full of darkness and Jake could see it threatened to devour her.

Lucy had lost her battle with that inner darkness, and Jake could see that Anna was very close to losing her fight as well. He would not let that happen.

"I didn't know you have a sister," Helmut said. "What is her name?"

"Her name was Lucy," Jake said, not emphasizing the past tense, but Helmut noticed. "She died almost two years ago."

Helmut was unusually quiet; no smart comment seemed to be forthcoming.

"I'm sorry, Jake," he said.

Jake just nodded.

Helmut was a good person, and Jake knew he could share his sad story with his friend, but now was not the time. He could not look to the past when he had to deal with the difficulty of the present. Jake felt he was always just a step or two ahead of the tragedy he'd left behind.

"Anyway," Jake said, attempting to interrupt the now-uncomfortable silence. "Why is Anna avoiding me?"

"Maybe she's not. Maybe she just lost her phone or turned it off or something. I wouldn't worry so much."

"She broke up with her boyfriend, tried to kill herself, found out her boyfriend didn't kill himself but was instead murdered, and now she is a suspect. I think it calls for at least a little bit of worrying, even for you."

"Bah!" Helmut said. "It sounds like my final year of high school."

Jake looked at Helmut, a bit stunned before his big German friend started laughing.

"You are too easy, my friend," Helmut said. "Too trusting. That is why you are in this mess in the first place."

"You're probably right."

Jake stood and took his cereal bowl to the kitchen, then grabbed his hooded sweatshirt from the back of a chair.

"I guess I'll just run over to her place and see if she is there. If she calls here, tell her where I went."

"I think you're forgetting something," Helmut said. He picked up Jake's phone from the end table. As he was about to pass the phone to Jake, it chirped his message tone.

Helmut looked at the screen.

"From Anna." He tossed the phone to Jake.

He opened her SMS and read it, puzzled. "She wants to meet me in the science building, down in the basement where the old labs are."

"Romantic," Helmut said.

Jake ignored him. "I'm not even sure where that is. Why in the hell does she want to meet there?"

"I don't know," Helmut shrugged. "It's quiet and no one goes down there. Maybe she's being followed? Maybe hiding from Schmidt?"

Jake thought Helmut might be on to something. Maybe she was in trouble. Maybe Anna had spent the morning avoiding Professor Schmidt—but if that were the case, why wouldn't she answer Jake's calls? Certainly the professor knew where she lived, or at the very least could easily find out from her student records. Jake knew he had to get to her.

"Do you know where it is?" Jake asked, sitting next to Helmut and opening his laptop to Google Maps.

"Sure. Hand it over."

CHAPTER TWENTY

ONE OF THE PRIMARY SCIENCE buildings of the University of Vienna sits sandwiched between Boltzmanngasse and Währingerstrasse, within sight of the checkpoints and guards of the American Embassy in the ninth district of Vienna. The building houses offices, classrooms, and laboratories dedicated to the study of physics and chemistry.

Jake made the quick walk from his apartment. He had passed by this building many times before, but had never actually been inside since he had no classes there. Further down Boltzmanngasse, he could just see the American flag flying over his embassy. He idly wondered if Tess was working at this location. He realized how little he knew about her job.

He reflected again on just what a strange location Anna had chosen to meet. Perhaps Helmut had been correct—maybe Anna feared she was being followed and this was somewhere they could talk without being spotted. Jake had tried to figure out if he was being followed, but it wasn't as easy as it looked in the movies. Any time he thought he saw someone suspicious and looked at them, they looked back, probably wondering what his problem was. He had taken a circuitous route to the building, but really had no idea if anyone had tailed him.

It also could be that all of this cloak-and-dagger nonsense was in his head. Perhaps Anna had a class in this building and it was convenient for her to meet in the basement lab. He had to admit that was probably more logical. Until he actually had a chance to speak with her, though, he wouldn't know. Immediately after receiving her text he had tried calling, but there had been no answer. He also sent a text, but received no reply.

He thought she could have been in class or a meeting, but he found it odd and a little bit disconcerting that she couldn't take the time to send him even a one-word response. Even a simple "Later" would have gone a long way to putting him at ease.

The building had chosen was unremarkable. It was gray stone with carved ornamentation, the same as hundreds of buildings throughout the city, many of which had been rebuilt following the destructive Allied bombing campaigns during the final phases of WWII.

Approximately a hundred feet away stood a modern, tall steel fence around the front of the American Embassy. A booth stood at the end closest to Jake, a few armed guards positioned nearby. One was in the process of checking a car awaiting entrance. Jake watched the man circle around the vehicle, checking the undercarriage with a mirror on a pole while simultaneously swiping the hood release, door handles, and fenders with a little piece of paper. Jake assumed it somehow detected explosive residue.

After a few minutes, the guard went to the booth and the gate slowly opened. The car pulled forward only to be trapped by a heavy ramp, currently set in a vertical position. After the exterior gate was completely closed, the interior ramp lowered, allowing the car access to the compound.

To Jake it felt odd to see this level of security in such a calm, peaceful city as Vienna. He thought about every action movie he'd seen, where the hero ran into the American Embassy in order to seek sanctuary. It didn't look like anyone would be running into this embassy too quickly, especially if they were being chased by AK-47-toting terrorists.

Jake saw one of the guards look his way and he quickly turned to the physics building. He entered through the large wooden doors and got his bearings. A small guide on the wall listed the various classrooms, offices, and laboratories of the building and indicated their floors. On a floor listed as -1, it said *Labor*, or laboratories. A small piece of paper had been taped next to it but was now ripped down, only two taped corners still hanging. The paper was nowhere to be seen.

He found the stairs and went down. Both the stairwell and the corridor it led to were dimly lit, with most of the illumination coming through small windows to the outside. Today was Sunday, and although the building was open so that students could come and do any research they may need, there were no classes and most of the teaching staff had the day off. The building was very quiet, and he didn't see anyone else as he walked into the basement.

The room smelled old, and Jake could taste the mildew on the air. Although the main body of the building must not have been renovated in twenty years, it felt as though no one had updated this level since the war. He saw a few large buckets of paint and some brushes. Perhaps a refurbishment was planned.

The main hallway was dark, but Jake located a nearby light switch. After a few seconds of sputtering, the overhead fluorescents came to life and bathed the hall in an artificial light reminiscent of the giant box stores of his homeland. Halfway down a dead-end hall, Jake found the room labeled as *Labor A*. A light could be seen inside through the frosted glass of the door.

He opened the door and saw Anna sitting on a work bench, her feet dangling about a foot from the ground. She smiled when she saw him.

"Jake! Finally! You're late."

He momentarily forgot his annoyance at her lack of communication, and couldn't help but smile back.

"Sorry," he said. "I've never been here before and I wasn't quite sure where it was."

"It's so mysterious," Anna said. "I have a physics class on the second floor, but I've never been down here. I thought it was closed for construction."

Jake was puzzled by her statement. He also didn't understand her attitude of expectation, as though she awaited something from him.

"Why did you want to meet here?" Jake asked.

A small frown shadowed her face. "I didn't," she said. "I mean, I wanted to meet with you, but you picked the location."

"No, I didn't. You sent me a text—like a half hour ago, you said to meet here."

"Are you trying to scare me, Jake?"

"I'm dead serious," he said.

He pulled out his phone and showed her the text, the caller ID clearly showing her phone number and name. She took the phone in her hands, but her grasp was weak and Jake snatched it before it fell from her fingers.

"I lost my phone," she said. "I haven't seen it since soon after you came by my apartment. I've been looking everywhere for it."

"If you didn't send the text," Jake asked, "then who did?"

She shook her head. "Helmut called me. He told me you wanted to meet here, but that you were busy and asked him to call."

"Helmut?" Jake asked. "When was this?"

"About an hour ago," Anna said.

"I was with Helmut. He didn't call you. Why would he? None of this makes any sense."

"I'm getting scared, Jake," she said. "Why were we both told to come here?"

That was the real question. It took a second to sink in: someone wanted both Jake and Anna to meet in this place—this very quiet and deserted place. Jake's heart rate had already been high, but now it exploded like a rocket.

"We need to get out of here. Right now."

He grabbed Anna by the elbow and turned toward the door. He pulled her along with him quickly, too roughly, but she didn't complain. As he pulled open the door to the laboratory and turned into the hall, a small part of his brain had just enough time to register the quick single tone of a beep, similar to what one might hear on an alarm clock or a kitchen timer. A roar of sound and light and fire flooded Jake's senses briefly, and then everything went dark.

CHAPTER TWENTY-ONE

THE CALL HAD COME ONLY thirty minutes earlier, but Tess was already at the front of the ugly brown stone edifice of the Vienna General Hospital. It was the largest hospital in Europe and erupted like two brown moles from the otherwise porcelain skin of Vienna. She walked through automatic doors and went to the registration desk.

A nurse in pale green scrubs was sitting behind the desk.

"I'm looking for the room of Jake Meyer," Tess said, first in English and then repeating in German to make certain the woman understood. "I'm with the American Embassy."

The woman made a few clicks of the mouse and looked at her computer screen.

"Floor six," the attendant said. "I do not know that they will let you see him, but you can check at the desk."

Tess nodded and went toward the elevator. It was unusually large for Vienna, but built big enough to hold a gurney and a team of medical providers. She entered the lift with several other people, mostly workers, and hit six on the panel.

Shortly after the explosion, Tess had received a text alert from the embassy's emergency warden system warning that an explosion had occurred in the vicinity of the compound. It had been at least another hour before she learned that Jake had been in the lab at the time. According to the police, preliminary investigations suggested that it was not a terrorist attack, but rather an accident in the physics lab, probably caused by ongoing renovation in the building.

A representative from the hospital had called first, telling Tess that two students had been injured in the blast and one was an American. After learning it was Jake, she quickly grabbed a jacket and took off for the hospital.

The elevator doors opened and another small reception area stood before her, a different nurse sitting behind the computer.

"I'm from the American Embassy," Tess said. "Here to see Jake Meyer."

The nurse looked at her, but didn't say anything. She started flipping through some charts on the counter.

"He was in the explosion today," Tess added.

"Ah, yes," said the nurse. "Room 603 on the right."

Tess turned to go, but then stopped and turned back to the nurse.

"Is Anna Duerning also on this floor?" The nurse once again began to check her files. "She was with Mr. Meyer and also injured in the explosion."

"Oh," said the nurse. "No, I'm afraid the young lady suffered injuries more severe than Mr. Meyer. She should be on the second floor somewhere. Mr. Meyer was quite lucky, in fact. It would be best if he stayed the night for observation, but he can leave any time."

Tess thanked the nurse and went to find Jake's room. The door was closed, but she cracked it open a few inches and knocked.

"Jake? It's Tess."

"Come on in," he said from inside the room.

She closed the door behind her and entered the dimly lit room. Jake was lying on the bed, but propped up to a nearly seated position. He wore a flimsy hospital gown and had a scratchy-looking yellow blanket pulled to his chest. It didn't appear he was hooked to any sort of equipment or an IV.

Apart from a few butterfly bandages on his face and some white bandages wrapped around his right arm, he looked shockingly well for someone who had just survived a gas explosion.

Jake smiled when he saw her, and she had to admit to herself that she was glad to see him again, as well.

"Thanks for coming," he said. "How did you hear? I lost my phone in the explosion."

"American blown up overseas? That's sort of my job."

"I see," he said with a smirk. "So it's a professional visit. Are you going to update my member of Congress?"

"Professional and personal." She smiled at him. "How are you feeling? You look really good, actually."

He smiled and Tess felt the blood rush to her face.

"I mean for someone who was blown up this morning."

Jake laughed. "Actually, apart from a pretty killer headache, I don't feel too bad. I've got some burns on my arm, but otherwise it's just a few bumps and scratches."

He was quiet for a moment as Tess stood by his bedside. In the background he had the television on, but muted. An old episode of *Law and Order* played, no doubt dubbed in German.

"They won't tell me anything about Anna," he said at last.

Tess felt a momentary flash of jealousy, and was angry with herself for it. Of course he was worried about his friend; she could have been killed. *Perspective, Tess.*

"The nurse told me she is on another floor," Tess said. "I guess she was hurt a little worse than you. I can try and find out more."

"Thanks," Jake said. "I would really appreciate it. They won't tell me much about anything that happened, actually."

"What do you remember? Why were you down there in the first place?"

"It was Professor Schmidt, Tess," Jake said, his brown eyes hard. "He tried to kill us."

"Wait, hold on a second. What are you talking about? The police are saying it was a gas explosion caused by construction. What does Schmidt have to do with it?"

Jake explained his earlier failed attempts to reach Anna before suddenly receiving her text and the meeting request. When they'd both arrived and neither had actually contacted the other, Jake had known something was wrong.

"I never expected a bomb was about to go off, but I knew if someone had lied to get us both in the same place, it couldn't be good. I wondered why Anna would want to meet in such a deserted location. Now, it's obvious."

"It's very strange," Tess said. "I'll give you that."

"Strange? Tess, someone tried to kill us. If I had waited two seconds longer we would have been standing in the middle of that room when it exploded, instead of being in the hallway outside. We'd be dead."

He was sitting up higher in his bed, the blanket falling down to his waist. Tess held up her hands in a universal gesture of calm.

"Just hang on a second, Jake," she said. "Of course I'm happy you weren't in that room when the explosion happened. I just don't know that we have proof that Schmidt was behind this."

"Who else could it be?" His voice began to rise.

"I don't know," she said. "But we don't really know much, do we? We don't know that Professor Schmidt is in love with Anna. We don't know that Christian wasn't into something shady. This is all just speculation."

She could see the muscles around Jake's jaw tightening. Tess softened her tone and rested a hand on his leg. "Maybe you're right, but we can't prove it. Why would Schmidt want to kill you guys? You told me he was in love with Anna."

"Think about it. He knows I know Christian died in his office. He's seen me with Anna a few times. Maybe he thinks she's a lost cause. Or maybe he sees me as his newest competitor. The guy is crazy, Tess."

"That's a lot of maybes."

"I thought you wanted to help me."

"I *do* want to help you," Tess said. "But this isn't a movie. We need to take this to the police. If you think Schmidt was behind this—if you really think it wasn't an accident or just a really terrible coincidence—we need to tell someone."

"I told you, Tess," he started very loudly, before dropping his voice. "I can't go to the police. Not yet. I lied to them once. Why would they believe me now?"

Tess sighed and spoke before she could stop herself. "That was a really dumb thing to do, Jake."

He looked hurt. Jake pulled the blanket back up to his chest. She regretted the words. It was true, but now wasn't the time to rub his nose in it.

"I know it was. I made a stupid mistake, but I know Anna didn't kill Christian. If you don't want to help me, then maybe you should just go."

"I didn't say that," Tess said. "Maybe you should rest a little bit and we can talk later."

"Yeah," he said.

Tess suddenly remembered she had duties as a consular officer, as well.

"Did you want me to contact your family for you?" She pulled a piece of paper from her bag. "I'd need you to sign this privacy act waiver…"

Her voice trailed off. Her sudden switch to her bureaucratic language sounded lame even to her own ears.

"No, thanks. I'm feeling tired. Thanks for stopping by."

He didn't look at her, his eyes focused on the television in the corner of the room.

Tess could take a hint. She packed her bag back up. "Sure," she said. "You rest, and I'll check on you later."

Jake didn't say anything, and continued to watch the silent television program. Tess left the room and closed the door behind her.

CHAPTER TWENTY-TWO

JAKE SAT IN THE HOSPITAL bed, the lawyers on his television show making their final arguments. It turned out the helpful friend from the beginning was, in fact, the true killer. He wished his own murder mystery was so simple.

He was angry with Tess. Why couldn't she see what was so obvious to him? Professor Schmidt had to be behind everything. He killed Christian. He then tried to kill Anna and Jake as they began to get too close. Or maybe he tried to kill them because he was jealous.

Jake admitted that he didn't have everything completely worked out, but his fundamental solution had to be correct. Schmidt was trying to kill him-he could feel it. Now, he just needed to prove it.

By now, the professor would have learned that he and Anna had survived the explosion, and he might be looking for a way to finish the job. Jake knew he would have to act fast if he didn't want to end up like Christian. While he could certainly overpower the old professor in a fair fight, it didn't seem that was the way Schmidt operated. The explosion had been too close.

There was a light knock at his door.

"Come in."

The door opened and Helmut and Mira came in. Helmut had his usual cheerful look plastered on his face, but Jake knew his friend well enough to see it was forced. Mira didn't attempt to hide her concern.

"Jake," Helmut said. "You look awful."

"Shut up, Helmut," Mira said. "How are you feeling, Jake? What happened?"

"I'm fine. Lucky, really. We had just left the room when it exploded. Thank God for solid Austrian craftsmanship, I guess."

"Helmut told me about your text message. What did Anna say?"

"She said she lost her phone a day or so earlier. She was there because she had a call from Helmut telling her to meet me at the physics lab."

"That's not true," Helmut said immediately. "I've never spoken with Anna on the phone. I promise you, Jake."

"I know," Jake said. "Don't worry about it. You and I were sitting in the living room together at the time she said you called her. It couldn't have been you."

"It wasn't!" Helmut insisted.

"Though you did leave the room to go get something from the kitchen, as I recall…" Jake said, playfully prodding his friend.

Helmut started to sputter and turn red in the face. Jake went easy on him.

"I'm joking, Helmut," he said. "I know you didn't call her, but someone pretending to be you did. Someone who wanted both of us in the lab."

Helmut seemed ready to speak again, probably with a terrible joke, but Mira cut in.

"Jake, this is serious."

"You think I don't know that?" he asked. He waved his hands to indicate the room around him, but winced in pain at his burned right arm. The doctors had said the burns were minor, but they hurt like hell. Apparently that was good. If it didn't hurt at all, that was supposed to be a very bad sign. If that was the case, he figured he must be in great shape.

"I'm freaked out," he continued. "Someone tried to kill me. Someone else is already dead. Anna is…"

Jake suddenly realized he didn't know how Anna was doing. He knew she was alive but on another floor, and had required more treatment.

"I need to find out about Anna," he said.

Jake started to rise, but Mira stepped in front of him and gently put her hands on his shoulders.

"You need to stay in bed," she said. "Helmut will find out about Anna."

"I will?" he asked, eyebrows raised.

"You will," Mira said.

Helmut opened his mouth, but at a look from Mira thought better of it. He shrugged, turned, and walked out of the room.

"Honestly, Mira. I'm fine. A few burns and scrapes, but the doctors said I don't even have to stay if I don't want. If this was an American hospital, they would have kicked me to the curb by now."

Mira sat on the bed next to Jake and shushed him. "It's not about that," she said. "I needed to get Helmut out of the room. We only have a few minutes."

"What are you —" Jake said, but Mira cut him off.

"I have an idea what this is about. Well, not exactly an idea, but I think I know what started everything."

"Something with Christian?"

Mira nodded. Her green eyes were sharp and focused, the same look she had while writing papers for her classes.

"During the time Christian and I were…together," she said, "he found a photograph that I usually keep in my room."

"What is the photo?" Jake asked.

"I'm getting to that," she said. "Don't interrupt."

Jake was used to Mira's rather direct manner and knew not to challenge her.

"The photo is very dear to me. It is a picture of me as a little girl—probably only three—with my mother and my uncle. It is one of the very few photographs that I have of my mother. She died many years ago."

Jake had never known this, but had long suspected Mira was orphaned. Her uncle was clearly a guardian of sorts, but she never mentioned the rest of her family. Jake wasn't very informed about the wars that took place in the former Yugoslavia, but he imagined there were a lot of damaged families from this tragic time.

"One day when Christian was over, he saw this photo and asked me about it. It was very nice. At first. I told him about my family. I talked about my mother and what I remembered. I spoke of Serbia. I told him about my uncle and how I came to be in Vienna."

Jake realized how little he knew about Mira. Though friendly, she was a tough puzzle to solve. She didn't easily open up and when he was with her, Helmut was usually present as well. Helmut was always able to fill any gaps of silence long before Mira had a chance to start.

"What changed?" Jake asked.

"I don't know," Mira said. "I remember I was telling a story about the time mother and I went to the market when suddenly Christian stood, like he had been shocked. I asked him what was wrong, but he wouldn't tell me."

"He didn't say anything?"

"He said that he needed to go and that it was very important he check something. He wanted to borrow my photograph."

"And you let him take it?" Jake asked.

"I didn't want to. I cherish that photo, but I think he saw my hesitation and turned back to the charming Christian I fell in love with. I trusted him, Jake."

Jake was taken a little aback to hear Mira speak of love. He hadn't realized how much she'd cared for Christian. From Mira's perspective, it was clearly more than a fling.

"He did that smile he did—you wouldn't know, I suppose—but he did it, and I agreed. He promised to bring the photo back in a few days. It was soon after that our relationship fell apart. I don't know what happened, but he decided he wanted Anna. I couldn't get him to talk about anything, the photograph included."

Jake thought about it. It was strange certainly, but he didn't see the connection between an old family photo of Mira's and Professor Schmidt blowing up a physics laboratory.

"I don't know how that could have anything to do with what is going on now," he said.

"But it must," Mira said. "Everything changed after he saw that photograph. He went back to Anna. For the first time, I heard him mention Herr Professor Rudolph Schmidt."

Jake sat up at the mention of the professor. "He talked about Schmidt? What did he say?"

"It was the next day. He asked if I knew him, and I said I didn't. He seemed angry and I didn't understand why. He became very agitated. He didn't believe me."

"That is weird," Jake admitted.

"That fight," she said. "That was the last time we really spoke."

She looked sad, lost in thoughts of what could have been. Jake felt he should comfort her, but before he could decide how, the door opened.

"Anna is on the second floor," Helmut said.

He looked at Mira sitting on the bed next to Jake. For a moment, he frowned before quickly attempting to cover it up with his normal broad smile.

"Looks like I missed something?" Helmut asked. "You two need a room?"

He laughed loudly, but it rang false to Jake.

"How is Anna?" Jake asked as Mira stood.

Helmut looked distracted, but answered. "She's stable, but she took a bit more of the blast than you. The doctors think she suffered a concussion in addition to some burns and cuts."

Seeing the concern on Jake's face, he immediately added, "She'll be okay, though. She will just have to stay in the hospital a few days."

"I'm going to find out why this happened," Jake said. "I promise."

"Not if you're behind bars," Helmut said. "Let the police do their work. Tell them what you know, but stay out of it. Your friend at the consulate isn't going to get you out of jail."

"Let's let him rest," Mira said, cutting Helmut off.

"Right," Helmut said. "We'll head home. If you stay the night and need us to bring anything, just give me a call."

"Thanks, guys," Jake said. "I really appreciate you coming by."

Jake knew he had no intention of staying a minute longer than he had to, but he didn't want to drag his friends into his mess. It was best they went home and he did what he had to do without their knowledge. Whatever that might be.

Mira and Helmut grabbed their jackets and said their goodbyes. As Mira gave Jake an uncharacteristic hug, she whispered in his ear.

"Find my photo, Jake."

CHAPTER TWENTY-THREE

JAKE WAS PULLING HIS SHIRT over his head, gingerly feeding his burned arm through the sleeve, when the nurse came in. She was startled to see him up and dressing.

"No," she said. "You must lay down."

"No," Jake said, fixing his collar. "I must not. I must go."

He was being rude and he knew it. He was the last one who should be mocking someone's less-than-fluent foreign language skills, but he couldn't be in this place any longer.

After Helmut and Mira had left, he'd pondered Mira's story. How could a photograph from her childhood lead to Christian's death and the attempted murder of Anna and himself? It made no sense, but he was sure Mira's instincts were correct. It had to mean something. It also provided an extra connection between Herr Professor Schmidt and everything that had transpired the last few weeks.

Before he did anything else, though, he needed to check on Anna—not only because he was worried about her, but also because she might know something about this mysterious photo, and Christian's reaction. If she didn't, at the very least she could tell him where Christian lived. That would be the first place to start hunting for this photograph. It felt like a needle in a haystack, but if it was the key to unlocking the mystery, he had to try.

The nurse decided Jake did not intend to get back into bed as told. When he started to put on his shoes, she turned and left the room without a word. He was confident they couldn't keep him here against his will, but at the same time he'd rather not have to argue with a doctor about it. He decided to get out quickly.

Opening the door and peering around the corner, he saw the nurse quickly walking away down the hall toward the desk at the end. Jake slipped out and went the other direction, searching for a stairwell or secondary elevator he could use to get to Anna's floor.

Jake moved with purpose, peering over his shoulder regularly. He knew he must look incredibly guilty, or at least suspicious. At any moment he expected cries of "Stop that man!" to erupt behind him, but they didn't come. He was just another young guy walking in the hall. He could have been one of any of the family and friends here to visit a patient.

He came to the end of the hallway and, as he'd expected, there was a stairwell. He started down the stairs, each step causing his head to pound harder. For a moment, he wondered if he should be leaving the hospital so quickly—after all, he had survived an explosion just a few hours earlier. Anna was suspected of having a concussion, though, and she was being kept longer and on a different floor. He guessed this meant the doctors thought he didn't have one. He would just have to find some aspirin and fight through the headache.

After going down four floors to reach the second level of the hospital, Jake was winded, but convinced no one was following him. He had passed a few others on the stairs, but none had shown any interest in him. He entered the corridor and realized he had no idea where to go. This floor had fewer rooms, the level of care presumably greater here with a higher staff-to-patient ratio.

He contemplated going by and peeking in all the rooms, but decided that would be far more suspicious than simply asking. He went to the staff desk, a mirror of the one on his floor four stories up. Two nurses sat there, but neither acknowledged him.

"Excuse me," he said. "I'm looking for Anna Duerning."

One of the two looked up at him, while the other kept working on her computer.

"Are you family?" she asked.

"Yes," Jake said. "Well, no. A friend actually, but she doesn't have family in Vienna. She will want to see me."

He tried to soften his features and look as puppy-dog as possible.

The nursed sighed.

"Down this hall and then take a right," she said. "Her room is 207, on the left."

He thanked her and started the way she'd indicated. As Jake turned the corner, he saw a familiar face in front of Anna's door talking on a phone. Without missing a beat, he pivoted and went back around the corner. It was Deputy Inspector Kurz, the female police detective who had visited him at home.

She must be here to speak with Anna about the explosion. If they wanted to talk to her, Jake knew he must be on the list as well. He needed to get out of the hospital. He wasn't ready to talk to them—not yet. Not until he had something to prove Schmidt was behind this.

He re-traced his path back down the hall to the information desk. The nurse looked up as he approached.

"Could you not find the room?" she asked.

"No, it's just…" Jake said.

He heard a woman's voice call out from behind him.

"Herr Meyer?"

He didn't look. He knew it was Kurz. The nurse looked down that way and saw the police officer. She looked back to Jake, suspicion clouding her features.

Jake didn't take the time to explain. He pretended not to hear Kurz, and turned to the main stairwell directly across from the desk.

The nurse behind him called out after him, but he was already taking the stairs two at a time. He did not hear Kurz call again, but he knew she must be following. Not pausing to look back, Jake made his way to the ground floor, silently cursing the European floor-naming conventions. Their second floor was the equivalent to a third story in the States.

Running down the stairs drew a lot of attention and, even worse, caused his head to throb to the point his vision was starting to blur. He had to get out of the hospital and to Christian's place to look for the photograph.

Finally reaching the ground floor, the large atrium surrounded him. He slowed to a very brisk walk, hoping people would stop staring as he moved toward the exit. He could see the sun shining outside. No one called his name from behind as he crossed the lobby.

He darted quickly through the automatic doors and collided roughly with Inspector Renner coming in from the outside.

For a moment, he thought he was going to black out. In addition to his splitting head, he had managed to smash his burned arm between their two bodies.

"Are you okay, Mr. Meyer?" Renner asked, helping to steady Jake.

Jake was too off-balance to react at first, but after a second he registered whom he had run into and started to pull away. Renner's hand closed like a vice on Jake's shoulder. The man was stronger than he looked.

"Not too fast," the inspector said. "After all, you do not want to fall and hurt yourself."

"Yeah," Jake mumbled.

"Funny I should run into you. My colleague just called and said she saw you. You must not have heard her."

"Guess not," Jake said.

"We heard about your terrible accident this morning. I am glad that you are okay."

"Thanks," Jake said. "Listen, I need to go."

Renner ignored Jake.

"In fact, it is shocking you weren't hurt worse. It was quite an explosion, I'm told. Your friend Anna was almost killed. You could have been killed, but it seems your luck is much better."

Jake didn't like the tone. It was friendly, but oozing with an undercurrent of accusation. He held up his bandaged arm.

"Not too lucky," Jake said.

"Well, that is nothing really though, is it? It could have been much worse."

"What exactly are you trying to say?" Jake said. He felt his face flushing and tried to slow his breathing.

"Nothing," Renner said. "It's just that some bad things have been happening lately and you always seem to be there when they occur. In my line of work, we notice these sorts of coincidences."

"I could have died," Jake said.

"Yes," Renner said. "But you didn't. What were you doing in that lab? You don't have classes there."

"How do you know?" Jake asked.

"Because I checked."

"Am I under arrest?" Jake asked. He felt uncomfortable being so blunt. It felt like something from a movie, but he had to gamble. He was losing control of this conversation.

Renner planted a look of feigned shock on his face.

"Arrest? Of course not. We're just talking. Talking about coincidences."

"I need to go, then. The U.S. Embassy has contacted my family. They'll be worried if I don't call."

Jake added a little extra emphasis to 'U.S. Embassy' in case it would give Renner pause. If it did, Jake couldn't tell.

"By all means," Renner said, stepping to the side. "After all, we can always talk more later. I know where you live."

Jake didn't answer. He turned to walk away and saw Kurz also come out of the front of the hospital. She fixed Jake with a hard look.

He nodded to Kurz, looked at Renner for a moment, and turned and walked quickly away. He could feel two pairs of eyes drilling into his back.

CHAPTER TWENTY-FOUR

MONDAY MORNING FOUND TESS BACK at her computer in the visa window. The waiting room was full, this always being their busiest day of the week. She did her best to ignore the expectant eyes fixed on her from the other side of the window as she prepared her work area.

Tess grabbed a handful of passports from the pile of applicants waiting to be adjudicated. She had been at the job long enough to recognize the cases with only a quick glance at the passports: burgundy for Austria and Germany; black for India and Iran; bright red for Switzerland. Any interest she'd once had in the designs was long gone now, after hundreds of interviews.

The first few applicants were a blur, simple renewal cases that required little thought on her part. Instead, she thought of Jake lying in the hospital bed. She understood he was angry, and also knew he had to be frightened. He was just being such a man about the whole thing, and it drove her crazy. This wasn't a movie. He wasn't expected to—he wasn't even *supposed* to—try and figure this out on his own. This was why there were police.

"Your visa is approved," she said to the woman on the other side of the window. "Take this ticket and come back in two days to pick it up."

As the visa applicant walked away, Tess grabbed the next passport from the stack. It was for a young Austrian student who wanted to go study at the University of Florida. She looked over his DS-160 visa application form and then flipped through his passport to get a feel for his travel history. Next, she entered his name into the various databases used to check for travel and criminal backgrounds.

Everything came back clear. It looked like a simple case. She called his name into the microphone and the student quickly approached the window, a file of papers in hand. He immediately started talking, but Tess cut him off. Visa officers controlled the conversation, not the other way around.

Her autopilot kicked on as she went through her typical list of questions, watched his reaction for anything unusual, and spoke with him a bit about his studies. Nothing out of the ordinary. By the time she had finished her questions, the results of the name check were on her computer, out of his line of sight. No criminal history. Normal travel patterns.

She marked his application as approved and handed him his ticket to pick up in two days.

"Go Gators!" the student said.

She was jarred from her thoughts. "I'm sorry?"

"Gators," the student said, suddenly self-conscious about whether he had used the right word. "Florida Gators?"

"Oh yeah. Go Gators." Tess did the two-handed Gator chomp she'd seen the students use during the football games. The student on the other side of the glass stared at her as though she had lost her mind. *Whatever.*

The student left and Tess finished up the process in her computer. She was about to clear out the database check when a thought occurred to her. Jake was so certain that Professor Schmidt was behind all this. It felt farfetched to her, but she reasoned that usually one doesn't just start stabbing and blowing people up out of the blue—there is a history. A history that she might have access to.

It was against every rule and regulation to do a name check on someone out of simple curiosity. These databases were some of the same used by the FBI and other law enforcement. This point had been hammered home repeatedly in consular training. In fact, several Foreign Service Officers had been terminated over the years for looking people up, often celebrities or ex-girlfriends and boyfriends.

Still, the rules were mostly in place to protect the privacy of American citizens, she reasoned. It wasn't very likely that Rudolph Schmidt was an AmCit. Use of the database was monitored and spot-checked, but Tess looking up an Austrian while serving in Vienna shouldn't raise any red flags.

If I find nothing suspicious, it'll help put Jake's mind at ease, she told herself. She knew she was justifying breaking the rules, but curiosity overwhelmed her.

Tess glanced casually behind her to make certain none of her coworkers were standing there. She could see Thurston in his glass-enclosed office talking on the phone.

She turned to the computer and typed *Rudolph Schmidt* into the database. She didn't have a date of birth, so she left it blank. It took a minute for the computer to filter through the millions of entries in the system. Tess ignored the applicants staring at her from the waiting area, clearly noticing that she was not currently with a customer and should be calling someone up. A few looked annoyed at her inaction.

After the hits started to roll in, Tess scanned the results. Several appeared to be Americans, and she carefully avoided clicking on those. One hit was a travel record from Austria to Cuba via Miami. She selected that record. There was a photo of Schmidt from Miami International Airport as he was processed by CBP. It looked like he had only transited en route to South America. Tess didn't know what Jake's Professor Schmidt looked like, but this guy appeared to be the correct age.

Using that record, she re-ran the search adding in the DOB. The results came quicker this time. She looked through the record and knew she had the correct man—his employer was listed as the University of Vienna. There wasn't much of a travel history, just the one transfer visa that he'd used in Miami. Of course, with an Austrian passport he was eligible to travel to the U.S. without a visa.

The strange thing was, there were no records before 1999. No travel, no criminal, no applications for a visa. It was like he'd been a shut-in before that point in time. She checked the aliases field, but it was blank.

There was one name in the known-associates field: *Radyslav Pritchko.* Tess clicked on that name and ran a new check.

Out of the corner of her eye, she noticed Thurston walking toward the visa line. She quickly minimized the database windows, grabbed a passport from her stack, and entered the name into the system.

"Hey, Thurston," Tess said, trying to keep her voice casual. "Busy morning?"

"Just the normal bullshit calls from the DCM," he said. "I guess we denied a visa to the housekeeper of some Austrian member of

Parliament. Far be it we enforce U.S. immigration laws if it might inconvenience the front office."

"Was it mine?" she asked.

"No, it was Sam."

She couldn't see Sam in the next window over due to the privacy divide, but she could hear him.

"Give me a break," he said.

"Don't worry," Thurston said. "I checked, and your adjudication was sound. I told the DCM as much. I told him if he wants to put his name on a referral form for some politician's Filipino housekeeper, then that's up to him. That shut him up."

Thurston stood for a moment. Tess wished he would go back to his office so she could finish her name check. She was certain he would somehow notice the minimized window on her computer screen.

"You guys need anything?" he asked.

"I'm good," Tess said. "Just a bit behind. My last student case was a little messy."

"I'm all right," Sam said. "Just trying to power through."

Thurston nodded and walked away.

Tess looked at the passport she had grabbed from her stack. It was Austrian, but the next one down was Serbian.

"Pritchko," she said quietly to herself. Serbian? Russian?

She glanced behind her, and then pulled up the name check screen again. She clicked on Pritchko's name and the results lit her screen up like a traffic light, mostly with a lot of red "Thou Shalt Not Issue a Visa to this Man" type warnings. The first thing she noticed was a permanent visa ban code she had never seen before: *3E(ii)* and *3E(iii)*. The second thing was multiple hits from the FBI database.

She looked at a reference sheet she had taped to the wall next to her computer with all of the visa ineligibility codes. The common ones she knew by heart, but a few were rarely used. She found *3E(ii)* and *3E(iii)* and checked her chart.

Participation in genocide. Commission of acts of extrajudicial killing and acts of torture.

"Holy shit," Tess whispered to herself.

Who the hell is this guy, and why is Professor Rudolph Schmidt listed as his known associate?

CHAPTER TWENTY-FIVE

JAKE HAD AWOKEN IN HIS own bed with only a fuzzy memory of how he had gotten there. He remembered his confrontation with Inspector Renner as he'd left the hospital, and had a vague recollection of his decision to go home first in order to shower and change. His head had been hurting so badly he decided to rest for just a few minutes to let the extra-strength Tylenol kick in. The next thing he knew, it was Monday morning.

He was angry with himself, but part of him knew he'd needed the rest. He was lucky the police hadn't come by to talk to him further after practically running from them at the hospital. Even worse was the time he'd wasted, but he had been in no condition yesterday for the tasks before him. He got into the shower, doing his best to keep his bandaged arm dry. The hot water stung the cuts on his face, but the pain diminished and the warmth brought clarity to his senses.

It was after nine a.m. and when he crept quietly from his room, he found the apartment empty. All three roommates had early classes on Monday mornings, so Helmut and Mira should be gone. Jake was missing his abnormal psych class, but considering he'd nearly been blown up yesterday, he thought the professor would give him a pass.

It seemed unlikely to Jake that Mira's missing photograph would be at Anna's place. Christian may have taken it there at some point, but she'd never mentioned it and if they had broken up, why would he have left it there? The most likely place for the photograph—if it wasn't in the trash somewhere in Vienna—was Christian's own apartment, but Jake didn't have a clue where that was.

The next-best option was Professor Schmidt's office. It was the last place Christian had been alive and, according to Mira, something about the photograph was connected to Schmidt, at least in Christian's mind.

Monday mornings were a busy time at the university, with many classes in session. Jake hoped that held true for Professor Schmidt, as well. If so, his office should be empty long enough to slip in and have a quick look around. If he found nothing there, he would have to get Christian's address.

~

Jake entered the main building of the University of Vienna at the corner of Universität Strasse and Schotten Ring. The busy Schotten Tor—Scottish Gate—U-Bahn stop stood opposite. A mix of tourists and locals made walking through the area a challenge. A large billboard stood in front of the university announcing the 650th anniversary of the institution, a ridiculous amount of time by American standards.

Like many old buildings in Vienna, the massive university headquarters had a series of interior courtyards. Here they had been remodeled in a modern design to now feature glass-enclosed elevators and stairwells. Jake went to the fourth floor, where he had previously found the office of Professor Schmidt—the same location where Christian had been stabbed, then pushed through the window.

Jake wondered if the police had questioned Professor Schmidt. Surely they must have. They had to know his office was a crime scene. Why hadn't he been arrested? All of the pieces were beginning to fall into place for Jake.

Schmidt must have been in love with Anna, regardless of their age difference. For some reason, Christian had decided to confront Schmidt on the issue. Schmidt stabbed Christian, perhaps in the heat of an argument. Panicking, he pushed Christian from the window and hoped it looked like a suicide. When he later saw Jake with Anna, his jealousy rose to new heights and he decided to kill both of them in the staged laboratory explosion.

Jake thought about it. Did it make sense? He wasn't sure it all held together. Christian had an affair with Mira. Was he so jealous as to go confront Schmidt? How in the world would a biology professor know how to rig a lab to explode? And what did Mira's photograph have to do with any of this?

He knew he had to find the photo. Hopefully, he would see what Christian saw and be able to connect the dots to Schmidt. Then, he'd reach out to Inspector Renner and confess to his earlier lies, but with the evidence needed to arrest Schmidt.

He found the fourth floor and, though not deserted, it was quiet. The floor was mostly office space, and Jake assumed most of the professors would be in class at this time. He stopped outside Schmidt's door and listened. It was quiet inside. He knocked two times and tensed, ready to rush off if he heard someone approach. There was no response. Jake tried the door, and was relieved to find it unlocked.

It was a good-sized office. The offices on the top floor of the main building were prized, and generally the most senior and respected professors and administrative officials occupied them. Before all this mess had started, Jake had never heard of Herr Professor Rudolph Schmidt, but clearly he had some standing in the university. Maybe it was protecting his reputation that had pushed him to murder, Jake thought.

There were several large bookshelves lining the walls, primarily filled with books on biology, chemistry, physics, and history. Most looked incredibly boring to Jake, but he had to admit they provided the sort of professorial feel the office needed. Jake noticed that there were no personal items; no framed photographs, diplomas, or mementos hung on the wall. The desk, too, was devoid of sentiment, with nothing beyond a basic university-provided PC and a few tablets of papers with illegible scribblings on them.

Jake looked over the notes to see if anything jumped out at him. Most of the writing was impossible for him to decipher, and what he could read was in German that he didn't understand. Jake pulled open the drawers of the desk, hoping Mira's photograph was somewhere inside. Extra pencils, pens, paper clips, and other typical office supplies were all he found.

He tried to be quick but quiet, glancing up at the wall clock every few moments to watch time tick away. Jake knew Professor Schmidt could return at any second. Most classes ended on the hour and, if the professor was currently in a lecture, that meant he could show up very soon.

On the lower left-hand side of the desk was the largest drawer. At the front it held hanging files with labels that indicated they were filled with notes from his various classes. The folders were crammed forward, something in the back of the drawer taking up most of the space. Jake pulled the drawer open as far as it would go. In the back, on the bottom of the drawer, sat a small gray metal lockbox.

"Jackpot," Jake said quietly.

He tried reaching in to pull it out, but the awkward angle and the folders before it made it difficult to slip his hand in. Jake grabbed a handful of hanging folders and pulled them out, then set them on the desk to free up space. He was able to slide the lockbox forward and get his fingers around it.

He pulled it out and set it on the desk beside the file folders. The metal was cold and textured. Jake could hear things sliding around inside, but it didn't weigh much more than a pound. The box was locked, a skeleton-style keyhole at the front.

Jake did a quick, frantic search through the drawers again, looking for a key. There was nothing. He grabbed one of the paper clips and bent out an end so that it would fit into the lock. Usually these lockboxes had a fairly simple mechanism. Bending the end of the clip, he inserted it and tried turning it. He could feel it catch as it hit the metal lock inside, but the paper clip bent before the lock gave way.

Jake noticed the noise in the hall outside had started to grow. He looked up at the clock. In his focus on the lockbox, he had failed to notice that it was past time classes should be ending. Chances were good that Schmidt could return very soon.

Jake bent the paper clip back into its pseudo-key shape and tried again with the same results. Swearing to himself, he grabbed a second paper clip and tried to use them both at the same time, hoping the additional strength would turn the lock, but they just slid apart and tangled together.

"Damn it," Jake said.

The noise in the hallway was considerably louder now.

Screw it, he thought to himself. He grabbed the lockbox and decided to take the entire thing with him. He'd get it open later. Schmidt would surely notice it was gone, but Jake would cross that bridge when he came to it. He just hoped it had something incriminating in it, and not just a few euros that Schmidt wanted to keep safe. The last thing Jake needed was adding burglary charges to his problems.

"Too late for that, I guess."

He grabbed the stack of hanging files from the top of the desk and shoved them back into the drawer, then did a scan of the room to look for any other evidence that someone had been through the place. Grabbing the few bent paper clips, he tucked them in his pocket. He suddenly thought of fingerprints and for a moment thought about trying to wipe things off, but he had no idea what he'd touched at this point.

With luck, Jake thought, *I can get the box open and see what is inside and put it back before Schmidt even knows it's gone.* Even better, perhaps there would be evidence of Schmidt's guilt inside and he could take it straight to the police. Certainly they would overlook how he got his hands on it when presented with the greater crimes of Professor Schmidt.

He tucked the bulky metal box under the front of his jacket and peeked into the hallway. There were quite a few people walking around, mostly staff, but several students as well, probably visiting professors during office hours.

Jake pulled the door closed behind him and slipped into the passing crowds of people. As he turned the corner to go downstairs, he thought he saw Professor Schmidt's face for a moment on the elevator as the doors opened, but Jake turned and quickly took the stairs.

CHAPTER TWENTY-SIX

JAKE WALKED QUICKLY THROUGH THE university building, doing his best to hide the lockbox under the front of his jacket. After the third person eyed him curiously, he realized it would look far less suspicious to simply carry the box in his hands as though he owned it, and hadn't just stolen it.

He navigated the busy streets around the Schotten Tor U-Bahn until he made it to the comparatively quiet side-alleyways of his neighborhood. He was relieved to find the apartment still empty, his roommates probably still in class or out studying. Though Mira knew what he was looking for, he wasn't sure she'd be thrilled with his explanation of stealing from a professor. Plus, he figured at this point the less he could involve his friends, the better. It was bad enough that he found himself in such trouble, without dragging Mira and Helmut down with him.

Jake went to his room and put the box on his bed. He realized they had no tools that he could use to pry the box open, so he grabbed a butter knife from the kitchen. He locked himself in his bedroom and sat next to the box.

As he'd noticed in Schmidt's office, the box was light, probably not weighing much more than the metal it was made of. When he shook it gently, a few objects rattled around inside, most notably something that sounded like loose coins or other small metallic objects.

Jake wedged the tip of the knife between the lid and the locking mechanism. This was a step he couldn't take back—the box would be permanently damaged if he went forward. Taking a sharp breath, he started to pry the knife upward, using the leverage to work the lid open.

The lockbox was sturdier than he had imagined, and the tip of the knife began to bend. Using the gap created, he shoved a bit more of the knife inside, able to slide down further to a thicker part of the dull blade. He pushed harder on the knife handle and could see into the box through the gap provided. It was too dark to tell what was inside.

With one final, sudden jerk, he yanked the handle of the knife upward and the lock gave out with a loud crack. The lid flew open, a few coins sailing from the box.

He grabbed the coins first and gave them a look. They weren't euros. The writing looked Cyrillic, like Russian perhaps, but there were no symbols he recognized. He set them aside, not considering them very important at the moment.

Inside the box was a small, black leather-bound address book. The quality wasn't very high and it looked new. Flipping it open, the first fifteen to twenty pages were filled with the same difficult-to-read script Jake had seen on the notepads on Schmidt's desk. It appeared to be written in a mixture of German and Cyrillic, but even if he could have understood the words, the writing was almost too sloppy to read. It seemed to be some sort of journal. There were also dates listed in German, occasionally with notes under them.

Jake thought it had to be important, so he set it aside for further reading. Maybe with time and a dictionary, he could translate some of it. If he was lucky, there would be something incriminating.

Dear diary. Today I killed Christian. Next I will blow up Jake.

That would be really helpful.

There was a small piece of deer antler inside, well-worn as though quite old. Jake couldn't think of any meaning to it other than possibly a personal memento. Along with it was a toy car made of metal, the blue paint partially rubbed away from years of tiny hands pushing it along imaginary roads. He set it aside with the antler.

Finally, at the bottom of everything, was a small stack of photographs. One in black-and-white could have been Schmidt as a child with his parents. There was nothing marked on the back. A few other photographs were landscapes, one showing a small cabin next to a lake. These photographs were in color, but faded, and Jake guessed them to be at least twenty or thirty years old.

Mixed in with the other photos was the one Mira had described. There was Mira as a little girl. The same keen gaze was apparent even then. She wore a simple, probably handmade dress of pale yellow. Standing next to her was a young woman, almost the mirror image of Mira today. Mira's mother was caught in the middle of a laugh, an expression Jake rarely saw on Mira's typically serious face.

On the other side of Mira's mother stood a man in a military uniform. The slightest hint of a smile was on his lips. Jake wondered if the man had said something funny, or perhaps it had been the unknown photographer. The military man had an arm wrapped casually around Mira's mother's waist. The three of them stood in front of a small fountain in a town square. A few others could be seen going about their lives in the background.

Jake flipped the photograph over. In Mira's hand was written, *Me, Mother, and Uncle Slava.*

So this was the mysterious Uncle Slava who served as Mira's guardian. Jake had never seen the man, let alone met him. Mira rarely mentioned him and whenever he called, she took the call to another room. It was clear to Helmut and Jake that she had no desire to share that part of her life with them.

Jake turned back to the image on the photograph, struggling to figure out what Christian may have seen that could have caused him such excitement.

He looked carefully at her uncle's uniform. The style was unfamiliar, clearly a Serbian military uniform that Jake had never seen. There was nothing particularly unusual about it from Jake's perspective, though it did have several medals on it. Her uncle looked to be quite high ranking.

Mira's mother was pretty, very similar in appearance to her daughter, though her features were a bit less distinctive. Mira must have inherited her stronger jaw and brow from her father. Like her daughter in the photo, the woman wore a simple, likely handmade dress. Jake saw nothing unusual there.

Mira herself looked like most little girls, her eyes fixed on the camera and not her mother laughing next to her. She wasn't smiling in the photograph, but she also didn't seem sad or angry. She held a fistful of her mother's dress in her left hand.

Jake saw nothing suspicious or upsetting about the three—certainly nothing that could lead to murder. He examined the background.

The photograph wasn't very large, and the quality rather low. The camera was focused on Mira and her family, so the background was not particularly sharp. He could see what seemed to be a stone courtyard with some sort of fountain or statue in the center. It was difficult to make out the details. The front of a few buildings were visible, but the contrast was not high enough to determine anything more. There were a few figures in the background, mostly blurry, though a few could be picked out.

Jake brought the photo closer to his face. Just over the shoulder of Uncle Slava was a man who appeared to also be looking toward the camera. The man had clearly seen the photograph being taken, but had either not been quick enough to get out of frame, or didn't realize he was in the shot. If Jake hadn't known what he was looking for, he never would have seen it.

This second man had heavier glasses and darker hair than he wore today, but there was no doubt in Jake's mind: it was certainly Rudolph Schmidt. He stood perhaps a dozen feet behind the posing family, and most of his body was blocked from the shot, but part of his left chest and shoulder could be seen.

He wore a uniform very similar to that of Uncle Slava, but the quality of the photograph made it difficult to make out details such as rank or title.

Two questions immediately jumped into Jake's mind. One, why would an Austrian professor of biology be in a twenty-year-old Serbian village photo? And two…

"Why is Schmidt wearing a Serbian military uniform?" Jake asked quietly to the room around him.

Jake knew Christian had seen the same thing. He didn't have any idea why it would have upset Christian, but one thing was clear: Herr Professor Rudolph Schmidt had a secret in his past. If Christian had confronted the man about it, was it worth killing for?

CHAPTER TWENTY-SEVEN

TESS FINISHED THE REMAINDER OF her visa interviews before lunch. In the afternoon, Sam and Tess each had a special portfolio to manage. Sam was the non-immigrant visa chief—mostly by virtue of this being his second tour as opposed to Tess's first—and had a lot of administrative tasks to handle: checking the supplies, making sure all the cash matched up with the fees charged, that sort of thing.

Tess was responsible for immigrant visas in the afternoon. These cases were quite a bit more complicated, as they resulted in a green card to the United States, and eventually citizenship. She conducted three or four of these interviews every week.

She also served as the section's fraud-prevention officer. If this were West Africa, Central America, or Thailand, that might be a difficult job. However, she was in Austria and there was relatively little visa fraud here. Occasionally, she might have to run a name through LexisNexis or verify a document with the police, but all in all, her portfolio didn't keep her that busy.

Both of the visa officers sat in an open room, each in a corner. Thurston of course had a private office, as did David, the deputy head of the section and primary officer for American Citizens Services. Along with the four Americans, eight Austrians were on staff to help with administrative tasks. Most of them had worked for the American consular section for nearly as long as Tess had been alive.

Sitting at her computer, Tess tried to be as casual as possible as she checked to see who was behind her. Sam was focused on reconciling the day's visa issuances. She could see into Thurston's glass-enclosed office. He was on the phone.

She pulled up the CCD database and entered Radyslav Pritchko. It took a moment, but the same hits as earlier popped up on her screen. This guy was most definitely not to be issued a visa to the United States. He had several permanent bans in place. Tess wondered the point of multiple permanent visa bans, but she guessed it made as much sense as the multiple death sentences often handed down by judges in the States.

In addition to his travel restrictions, to Tess it appeared Pritchko also had international arrest warrants out. The law enforcement databases were often difficult for her to decipher. Honestly, it rarely mattered what they said. If someone had serious red flags through the FBI or Interpol, all she needed to know was not to issue them a visa. It was rare there was additional info requiring the consular officer to contact the embassy FBI attaché. It appeared this may be one of those cases.

Tess knew she couldn't do that, though. She didn't actually have Pritchko in front of her. In fact, she didn't even have any reason to believe he was in Austria. All she knew was that he was a known associate of a professor at the University of Vienna. A professor who had not applied for a visa and, therefore, Tess never should have run through the system. This was a big problem.

If Schmidt was associated with this guy Pritchko in any way, he was bad news. Jake's theory that the professor could have had something to do with both Christian's death and the laboratory explosion began to seem more plausible.

Tess entered Radyslav Pritchko into LexisNexis, after clicking the acknowledgement that the service should be utilized for authorized use only. While that loaded, she did a Google search for the name. She was surprised to see Google return with some solid-looking hits almost immediately.

She scrolled through the first page of results and saw that he even appeared in a Wikipedia article. She clicked there first. Radyslav Pritchko didn't have an entry of his own, but he was mentioned in another entry titled "The Massacre at Foça."

~

As Tess read through the online article, she felt her stomach churn at the gruesome details of this particularly dark stain on humanity from the Yugoslav War. Foça had been a village in Bosnia occupied by Serbian forces. What had taken place there was later considered acts of genocide by the International Criminal Court.

She read with increasing horror, descriptions of public executions and rapes, mass graves, and townspeople tortured and imprisoned. Foça epitomized some of the worst of the brutality in this terrible civil war. At the end of the article, a series of Serbians were listed who had been tried by the ICC, some in absentia.

Among them was the name Radyslav Pritchko. He was accused of murder, kidnapping, and unlawful imprisonment. The court had sentenced him to nineteen years, but a note indicated he had never been captured, along with several others found responsible.

Tess returned to her Google search results. Most of the other results were either scholarly articles about the war or newspaper stories from the Balkan region. Even with Google Translate, it was difficult to understand many of the articles and none were recent. They repeated the history from the encyclopedia entry.

She looked at LexisNexis. There were no records of Pritchko since the massacre at Foça. He had obviously gone into hiding. Looking at his known-associates and relatives sections, she found several other men, many of whom were listed as deceased. For family, it seemed Pritchko's wife had long since passed away and they had no children. He had a brother, also deceased. The only living relative was a Mira Vladic, currently living in Vienna.

Tess jotted the name of Pritchko's niece down in her notebook.

What does this guy have to do with Schmidt? she thought.

In everything she'd read, there had been no mention of a Rudolph Schmidt. Were they friends? Had Schmidt once lived or studied in Serbia, perhaps? Obviously, some brainy analyst at the FBI had figured it out, as Schmidt's record in the system listed him as a possible associate to Pritchko.

There was only one way she was going to figure it out, but she knew taking the next step meant she was fully committed. If all of this turned out to be nothing but a web of paranoia on Jake's part, she could be killing her career. She had already improperly used the State Department consular database system. That alone could get her fired. Now she was contemplating bringing the FBI into it.

She opened the embassy phone directory on her computer and found the small section for the Department of Justice. At the top of the list was Steven Berk, the embassy's legal attaché, who was also an FBI agent.

She called the number and a secretary answered. Tess introduced herself and asked to speak with the LEGATT.

"Berk speaking," he answered, his raspy smoker's voice instantly recognizable.

"Hey, Steve," she said. "It's Tess. I'm working on a possible interesting fraud case and I was wondering if you have a few moments to help me understand an FBI hit in the system."

"Sure," he said. "I'll be in the office all afternoon. Come by whenever you want."

She knew that he was well aware that any discussion of criminal history was likely to be classified, or at least sensitive, and would have to take place in Berk's office at the main embassy chancery.

"Sounds great," Tess said. "I'll head over now. Be there in twenty or so."

"See you then."

Tess hung up and looked at the name Rudolph Schmidt on her screen one more time. Most of the information was blank, apart from the known-associates field—which read Radyslav Pritchko.

"This is such a stupid idea," she said to herself as she grabbed her purse. She sighed. It was pointless pretending her mind wasn't already made up. She spoke again, this time loudly enough to be heard. "I've got to run to the chancery."

Sam gave a grunt, but didn't look away from his screen. As she passed by Thurston's office on the way, her boss looked up at her from his phone call. She gave him a friendly wave, but didn't stop to explain where she was going.

~

FBI Legal Attache Steve Berk wasn't exactly forthcoming when Tess went to his office. Her colleagues in law enforcement and intelligence loved their secrets. Often it felt they flaunted their knowledge without ever revealing anything. It was incredibly frustrating.

Berk seemed to be a good guy, though she'd only met him a few times at various embassy functions. He was about the farthest thing possible from Hollywood central casting when it came to the mold of FBI special agent, but much more in line with reality. Berk was in his late fifties, with a bit of a belly and probably no chance of running down a fleeing suspect. Still, his intelligence was clear and he appeared to have a finely honed bullshit detector. Tess was sure she set his alarm bells ringing the moment she started talking.

"Is this really about a visa case?" he asked after she got to his office, where awards and photographs of Berk with the president and various members of Congress decorated the walls.

Tess didn't want to tell him everything. At least, not yet. She needed to know more herself before she admitted to abusing her position and running names through a protected criminal database.

"Not a visa case," Tess said. "No. An ACS case. I've got an American who seems to be in a bit of trouble and I'm checking over his story."

"What sort of trouble?"

There was little room for humor in Berk's eyes. As a low-ranking consular officer thirty years his junior, it was tough not to spill everything. He had refined that look over years of interrogations with criminals far tougher than Tess.

"I'm not sure yet. It's just a gut instinct at the moment. I want to look into it a little bit more before raising any red flags. It could be the guy is just a crackpot, and I don't want to get everyone spun up over nothing."

Her cautious, no-drama approach appeared to comfort Berk. He nodded and hit a key on his computer.

"I can respect that." He looked at his screen for a moment. "I've got to say, though, if you start throwing the name Radyslav Pritchko around too loudly, things are going to get serious real quick."

"Yeah, I sort of figured. His name popped up with a permanent visa ban associated with war crimes and genocide. Not exactly a typical case, and precisely why I want to dig a little deeper before I say too much."

"This guy Pritchko is an international felon, Tess."

"I understand." Berk raised an eyebrow, but kept his mouth shut. "Really, I do. But it's my first tour, and I don't want to make myself look like an idiot by claiming something that might just be bullshit."

He looked at her and then back to his screen. He scrolled down a bit through information on the monitor she couldn't see.

"All right," he said. "But if you think you have any sort of line on this guy, you need to tell me ASAP."

"I will. I promise."

"What do you want to know?" Berk asked. It was clear he had no intention of simply handing over files she had no right to see.

"What does Rudolph Schmidt have to do with Pritchko? Their files are linked as possible associates, but I don't have any idea why. It's Schmidt I'm interested in."

Berk read to himself for a few minutes, occasionally clicking on other pages. Tess did her best not to fidget. She felt like she was in the principal's office awaiting punishment. She tried to remind herself that she belonged here. She was a commissioned officer of the U.S. Foreign Service. She had paperwork signed by the president and an appointment confirmed by the U.S. Senate. So why did she still feel like the irresponsible girl her parents took her for?

"It's tough to say," Berk said after a minute. "The Pritchko case goes back twenty years, and it isn't easy to connect all the pieces. My best guess is your guy Schmidt is connected to someone who is connected to Pritchko. Schmidt might not have done anything wrong."

"Guilty by association? That seems a bit harsh."

"Welcome to the post-9/11 world. Law enforcement really changed its thinking and techniques once we had to start dealing with these nebulous terror groups. A lot of that spilled into our cases. These groups are like a spider web. Sometimes it's tough to spot the spider, so we go for the fly."

"So maybe Schmidt is innocent?"

"No one's innocent, Tess. All I'm saying is Schmidt might not have anything to do with Serbian genocide. What does this guy have to do with your case?"

She considered how much to say. Tess didn't know how much danger Jake was really in. Was it paranoia? If Berk decided to start digging into the death of Christian and the explosion at the physical sciences building, it might only make things worse. It wouldn't take the FBI man long to put some pieces together and find out Jake had provided a false alibi to the local authorities. A large part of Berk's job here was to serve as a liaison between American and Austrian law enforcement. He wasn't likely to have much sympathy for Jake.

"I'm not sure yet. My case is just a simple welfare-and-whereabouts check, but the AmCit had a friend die recently and he thinks Schmidt knows more than he's saying. You heard about the student that fell from the window?"

"Yeah, I read about it in the paper. Stabbed first."

"That's him. How'd you know about the stabbing? They kept that out of the papers."

Berk raised an eyebrow. Clearly, he wasn't forced to rely solely on the newspapers for his intelligence.

"Anyway, my guy thinks this professor is involved. I told him I'd look into it. Just to calm him down."

"Don't be doing the job of the Austrian police, Tess."

"I'm not," she said quickly. "I just wanted to do a quick check so I can feel good about reassuring my AmCit. The only weird thing was this name hit on Pritchko, but it sounds like nothing."

She could tell Berk was dissecting her story in his head and finding flaws. He didn't say anything, but his gaze was unwavering. She stood up quickly and grabbed her jacket from the back of the chair.

"I appreciate your help, Steve."

He reached into an interior pocket of his suit coat and pulled out a card. It was white, with a gold embossed FBI shield on it. He gave it to Tess.

"You should hold onto this. If you find out more about Pritchko, you let me know."

"I will," she said, tucking the card into the front pocket of her pants. "Probably nothing, though."

"I'm serious, Tess. You call me if you need help."

He held her hand for a second longer than comfortable, and she saw the unspoken words in his eyes. *I know you're not telling me everything, but I'm going to let it go. For now.*

"I promise, Steve."

CHAPTER TWENTY-EIGHT

JAKE HAD TO SPEAK WITH Mira. Hopefully, she could shed a little more light on what the photograph meant, and why Rudolph Schmidt was in the background. He tried her cell, but there was no answer. If she was in class, he knew she wouldn't pick up. He decided it couldn't wait.

Shoving the lockbox and all of its contents except Mira's photo under his bed, Jake headed for Mira's class. They needed to talk and, for Helmut's sake, it was probably best to keep him as much in the dark as possible.

Mira had an upper-level journalism class on Mondays, and it was held in the same building from which Jake had earlier taken the lockbox. In addition to providing a large percentage of the office space for university staff, the main building was home to some of the largest lecture halls and gathering spaces.

As Jake walked up the wide steps of the main entrance, he nearly stumbled over his own feet when he saw Professor Schmidt coming quickly out of the building and straight toward him.

Jake pulled his phone from his pocket and turned his back on the professor in hopes the man wouldn't notice him. It seemed Jake needn't have bothered. Schmidt was moving quickly and was flushed from the exertion. He wore a long gray coat buttoned to the top, and a tweed cap. His lips moved slightly as he passed, as though mumbling to himself, but Jake couldn't make out the words.

Considering the man had to be in at least his mid-sixties, he moved with a speed and determination that belied his age.

Jake took a quick look up toward the university entrance, but decided to follow Schmidt. At worst, he was headed home and Jake would find out where the man lived. At best, Schmidt would lead him toward something incriminating that Jake could take to the police.

He stayed back about thirty feet, worried he would lose the professor in the crowd around the U-Bahn station. Schmidt went down the steps, headed toward the U2 line. There was enough of a crowd waiting for the train that Jake could easily hide, but not so many as to lose sight of his target. Vienna was famous for its widespread and efficient public transportation. One almost never had to wait more than five or six minutes for a train or bus.

The purple-line train pulled in, headed in the direction of Karlsplatz. Jake entered the train one set of doors down from Schmidt. He kept his smartphone out, happy for the excuse to keep his face down in case the professor should look his way, but the man appeared lost in his own thoughts and barely registered the people around him.

After a few stops, the announcement for Karlsplatz sounded over the intercom in German. It was the end of the line and everyone had to exit, causing a minor crush of bodies near the doors.

As it cleared out, Jake looked around in a panic. He couldn't see Schmidt. The U-Bahn at Karlsplatz was huge, more of a mini shopping mall than a train stop. The professor could have gone above ground here or connected to other trains down different tunnels.

Jake moved to the center of the large space and looked for Schmidt's tweed cap among a sea of passersby. It was too chaotic. There were commuters, tour groups, and panhandlers moving in all directions at once.

Just as Jake thought he would have to give up his chase, he spotted the tweed cap as Schmidt walked briskly down the tunnel toward the U1 line in the direction of Reumannplatz. Jake jogged in that direction to catch up, but a large Italian family made it difficult to maneuver. He saw the train pulling to a stop ahead and knew he was going to miss it unless he ran.

He pushed through the middle of the family roughly. A shower of complaints accompanied with hands to the sky followed him, but he didn't have time to notice. He ran to the train and saw Schmidt getting on.

As the doors began to beep their warning and close, Jake reached them and jammed his arm inside. The door shut on his forearm hard, but its safety sensors made it reopen. Jake grabbed an empty seat, ignoring the few people staring at him. He risked a look further into the car and saw Schmidt standing with his back toward him. He seemed too lost in his own thoughts to notice Jake's pursuit.

They rode for several minutes. Train stops passed by and Jake read unfamiliar names. They were leaving the inner districts and heading farther out—to the tenth district, if he recalled correctly. There weren't many particularly rough parts of Vienna, but in some of the outer districts the city began to take on a bit more of a gritty, real-life-city feel, in contrast to the inner-city majesty of palaces and statues.

They came to Reumannplatz—the end of the line. All had to exit, but it wasn't as crowded as Karlsplatz due to the lack of tourists. Rarely would a visitor wander out this far.

Professor Schmidt continued to walk with purpose. It was clear he had a destination in mind. Could he live out this way? Jake thought it could be possible. He didn't know what he'd do if they came to Schmidt's house. He could wait until Schmidt left and try to get inside. Why not add another charge of breaking and entering to his growing list of crimes?

Schmidt took the escalator out of the station and Jake followed behind. The neighborhood around the stop was heavy with the influence of the immigrant communities of Austria. There were several Turkish restaurants, a Ukrainian grocery, a Russian bookstore, and mothers with their heads wrapped in scarves pushing children in strollers.

It felt a world away from Jake's ninth-district neighborhood of university students. After a few blocks of walking, Schmidt ducked into a small corner restaurant. There was no obvious name for the place that Jake could see. A Stiegl beer sign hung out front and another announced "Pizza" in faded letters.

The restaurant had small windows with curtains, making it impossible for Jake to see inside from his spot across the street. He found a nearby bench and waited. He couldn't risk going in while Schmidt was inside—the place was small, and there was no way he could enter without Schmidt's notice.

It didn't seem like a restaurant one simply stopped in to browse; this was a place where you were known or you came with someone known. He figured it was a family place that catered to one of the ethnic groups in the area.

Jake sat and waited, a few pigeons gathering around his feet hoping for handouts. As the minutes ticked by, he contemplated his next steps. Was the restaurant the final destination? Would Schmidt go home from here? Back to the university? It was still early Monday afternoon. Surely the professor either had another class to teach or office work. If Jake followed him back to school from here, what would he have accomplished? He needed to find out what was in that restaurant. It was too far to travel just for a meal.

After fifteen minutes, the door opened and the professor exited. He pulled his hat back on his head and adjusted the collar of his coat, which was crumpled and askew. It was difficult to tell from across the street and Jake couldn't risk staring too hard, but he thought Schmidt's face looked red, as though he'd been angry or fighting. Professor Schmidt began to walk back toward the train station, his pace slower this time, clearly no longer in a hurry. He shoved his hands deep into his pockets and kept his eyes on the ground. Jake probably could have stood right in front of the man and not been noticed.

Jake decided to let Schmidt go. He had to see if he could figure out who Schmidt had met in the restaurant. Snapping a quick photo of the outside with his phone, he crossed the street. The menu outside the door was mostly Italian food, with limited options. Lunch was as good an excuse as any, and he went inside.

~

The restaurant was dingy, years of grease and cigarette smoke coloring the tiled surfaces a dull gray sheen. The first thing Jake saw when he entered was a small display case with desserts, a few of which appeared to have been there a while.

Four small booths were to his left and one table for two to the right. Behind the display of apple cake and tiramisu was a bar, the liquor on the shelf leaning unusually heavily toward the vodka side of the alcohol spectrum.

A young woman with badly dyed raven hair and heavy eye makeup watched him enter, but didn't say anything. Jake took a seat at the table near the window and grabbed the menu. It was only one page of laminated paper, greasy like everything else in the room. He saw the same dishes as posted outside: lasagna, penne with peppers, gnocchi. They'd sounded good in the fresh air of the Vienna day, but now that he was inside, he'd lost his appetite, the taste of cheap cigarettes on his tongue.

He looked up and saw the woman behind the bar continuing to look at him. Jake smiled, but it did nothing to draw her in to take his order. She glanced to the other side of the room, where two men sat at the booth in the far corner. After a moment, as though she'd received telepathic approval, she walked over to Jake's table. She stood there, but didn't say anything.

"Coca-Cola, please," Jake said. He scanned the appetizers. The woman wasn't likely to talk if he didn't buy something else. "And, uh, the cheese plate."

He thought she rolled her eyes, but it was difficult to tell with the poor lighting and heavy mascara. She turned and walked away.

One of the men in the corner booth eyed Jake with violence. He was a stereotypical Eastern European thug—muscled build, but with a layer of fat on top. He wore a green tracksuit with white stripes, the front of the jacket open to reveal a tight black t-shirt underneath. His hair was cut short, and even from across the restaurant, Jake could spot the crooked oft-broken nose of a brawler.

The other man sat across from the thug, his back to Jake. He wore a lightweight Members Only jacket, his bald head surrounded by a wreath of white hair. He did not turn to see the outsider in the restaurant.

The waitress returned a few minutes later with a can of Coke, small glass, and a plate with an assortment of crudely cut cheeses on it.

"*Danke*," Jake said quietly. "*Sprechen Sie Englisch?*"

For a moment the woman looked frightened, her eyes clearly widening, visible despite the dark smudges around them. She shook her head briefly and turned to go, but Jake called out after her.

"I am supposed to meet my friend here," he said, continuing in German. "Have you seen him?"

The waitress stopped and turned to Jake, but quickly looked to the men in the corner. Without saying anything, she went into the kitchen.

He looked over at the men in the corner. The young man continued to stare Jake down, but made no move to get up. Which was good, because Jake was certain he had no desire to fight with Ivan Drago. Still, no guts no glory. Jake needed to know why Schmidt was here.

"Excuse me," he said, raising his voice so it would carry to the others. "Have you seen an older guy here recently? I was supposed to meet him."

The thug looked to the man across from him and raised a questioning eyebrow. Jake could almost see the thought bubble above his head. *You wants I should take care of him?*

"You are a friend of…" the older man said, his back still turned, "Herr Professor Rudolph Schmidt?" His voice sounded younger and stronger than his elderly appearance would have suggested.

The last half of the sentence was said with a smile that Jake could detect even without seeing his face. Behind the smile was sarcasm, but little warmth.

"Yes," Jake said. "Well, maybe not a friend exactly. An acquaintance."

He took a rapid gulp of Coke and steeled himself for whatever was about to come next.

The man across the room said something quietly in a language Jake didn't understand. The thug stood suddenly and Jake felt his stomach flip and the hairs on his neck stand on end. He looked to the door, ready to run, and gripped his pathetic little fork tightly.

The standing man motioned to his former seat. Jake stood and walked over. As he passed the front door it called to him, urging him to run, but he needed answers. This old man clearly had some.

Jake stood at the end of the little booth. The old man's muscular colleague stood the same height but still somehow loomed over him, his breath reeking of garlic.

"Please sit," said the old man. It was not a request.

Jake hesitated a moment, but a pair of heavy, calloused hands on his shoulders felt like the safety restraint of the world's worst roller coaster. Jake forced his knees to bend and landed hard on his ass, assisted by his new friend.

Jake knew instantly he'd just sat down across from Mira's Uncle Slava. The man was probably twenty years older than in the photo, but Jake had no doubt it was him. He was beginning to understand why Mira did whatever this man told her to do.

Slava was old, probably around seventy, but still seemed fit. His brown eyes were sharp and, though heavily lined with wrinkles, he had healthy skin. Jake couldn't say why, but the man made him think of his grandfather, long deceased.

Jake didn't have very fond memories of his grandfather. He was already confident he felt the same way about the man across from him now. It only took a minute to sniff out a bully.

"You just missed your friend, you know."

"I did?" Jake said. "That's too bad. I guess he forgot about our meeting."

"Too bad indeed. It is funny. I've never known Zorya to meet people in my restaurant."

"Zorya?" Jake asked. Was Mira's uncle thinking of someone else?

Slava chuckled and looked up at his companion, who smiled back stupidly.

"Sorry," Slava said. "I meant Rudolph. That is what he likes to be called now, yes?"

"Professor Rudolph Schmidt," Jake said. "Yes."

"And what were the two of you going to discuss in my restaurant?"

Jake had no idea. "Oh, I'm in one of his classes and we were just going to talk about some class…stuff."

Slava looked at Jake and peered through his obvious lies. A slight smile was still on his lips, but there was no warmth in his eyes. This was a man who got what he wanted. It was the same look he'd had in the photo; the absence of a military uniform did little to diminish his authority. His strength came from within, not from medals pinned on his chest.

"And since I missed him," Jake said, "I guess I will just pay and go. It was nice to meet you."

"No," Slava said.

Jake felt his heart skip a beat. For a moment, he couldn't breathe.

"I'm sorry?"

"No," Slava repeated. "We haven't met yet. My name is Slava."

Jake felt his tension release.

"I'm Jake. It was nice to meet you. I'll tell Herr Schmidt that you said hello."

Slava looked up at his sidekick once more and gave a slight nod. Before Jake had a time to register what had happened, his cheekbone smashed down onto the hard wood of the table in front of him. Stars appeared before his eyes and his vision dimmed before returning. The thug had a vicelike grip nearly three quarters of the way around the back of Jake's neck, pinning him to the table. His other hand smashed Jake's arm to his side.

"What the hell?" Jake managed to gasp.

Slava leaned across the table and whispered into Jake's ear.

"No. You will tell Zorya that I am not fucking around. He can bring me everything and maybe I will not kill him."

Slava reached into Jake's pocket and took out his wallet and phone and started going through both.

"I don't have any idea what you're talking about!"

The crushing grip on his neck tightened. For a moment, Jake thought the guy might actually be able to crush his vertebrae with one hand. He tried not to scream, but couldn't help it.

"I think you do," Slava said. He read from Jake's student ID card. "Jake Meyer. You will tell him to bring me everything, or I will start to hurt him. The first thing I will do is hurt those he cares about. It would seem you are on that list."

Slava grabbed a five-euro note from the inside of the wallet. "For your lunch."

His companion then dragged Jake from the booth, never relaxing his grip. He kicked open the front door with his foot and threw Jake out on the busy street. A few passersby watched as he fell hard to the concrete sidewalk, but at a look from the imposing man in the track-suit, they quickly continued on their way.

Jake stumbled to his feet and turned to the door. Slava stood there, his posture still as rigid as a soldier's.

He threw the wallet and phone at Jake's feet. "Tell Zorya this is not a game he wants to play. You tell him that, Jake Meyer, or next time I will let Dragan do things his way."

Jake took a few steps back as the door swung shut. Those around did their best to ignore what had just happened. It probably wasn't the first time someone had been thrown from Slava'a restaurant. Looking in through the window, he could see the Goth waitress coming out of the kitchen. They locked eyes. If there was any sympathy there, Jake didn't see it.

CHAPTER TWENTY-NINE

MIRA JUMPED TO HER FEET as Jake closed the door behind him. His khaki pants had a long asphalt smear along the right knee from his meeting with the sidewalk outside the restaurant. He limped slightly, trying to keep his pants from touching the raw scrape underneath.

"Jake, where have you been? I've been calling you."

He collapsed into the chair in the living room. He felt like he'd just gone ten rounds with Mike Tyson, even though he should have thrown in the towel after the first.

"What happened to you?"

"Where's Helmut?" Jake asked, looking around.

"He's at his study group. Never mind him. Where have you been? Why did you not answer my calls? Did you find my photograph?"

Each question was another nail pounded into his already-throbbing head. The burn from his arm was on fire, probably smashed on the sidewalk when he tried to break his fall. His week had quickly gone from promising to train wreck. One beautifully sunny Viennese morning he was at Café Strauss eyeing the pretty blonde next to him, and now he was being tossed from a restaurant by a Serbian thug. Oh, and yesterday someone had tried to blow him up.

He groaned in response to Mira's barrage of questions. "Give me a minute," he said. "It's been a rough day."

She got up, ran to the kitchen, and brought him a glass of water, half of which he quickly downed without a word.

"I've got good news and bad news," he said when he could finally speak.

"What has happened, Jake?" Mira asked.

He reached into his pocket and pulled out the old photograph and handed it to Mira. She closed her eyes and held it tightly to her chest, her lips moving slightly as though in prayer. Jake hadn't known her to be religious, but he was beginning to realize there was very little he knew about his Serbian roommate.

"The good news is, I found your photo."

"Thank you so much, Jake. How did you find it? Was it at Christian's apartment?"

"I don't know where Christian lives. You neglected to tell me and I got chased off by the police before I could ask Anna in the hospital."

"Chased by the police?" she asked. "What happened?"

"They seem to think I had something to do with Christian's death, and maybe even the explosion. I didn't like the questions they were asking, so I took off before they could decide if they wanted to arrest me."

"Oh, Jake…"

It was the same tone he'd heard his mother use in the past. "What was I supposed to do? I have to find some sort of evidence that Professor Schmidt is behind all this."

"But if you didn't find my photo at Christian's," she asked, "then where was it?"

"It was in Schmidt's office. And the only way he could have gotten it is if he took it from Christian, right?"

"I guess so," Mira agreed.

"It has to be. Which means Schmidt must have killed Christian. Nothing else makes any sense. Christian confronted Schmidt about the photograph. They fought and Christian ended up dead and the professor tried to hide it by pushing him out the window."

"I don't understand, Jake," she said. "What does a photograph of me as a child have to do with any of this? Why would someone kill Christian over that?"

"It isn't about you, Mira," Jake said. "It's your uncle. That's the bad news."

"What is the bad news?" she asked, her tone indicating she knew where Jake was headed.

"The bad news is your Uncle Slava is a royal asshole."

"Jake!"

"Maybe to you he is sweet Uncle Slava, but trust me, Mira, he is bad news. I'm not sure what sort of stuff he's into, but it's not good and it's definitely not legal."

Mira was quiet, looking at the creased photograph in her hands. When she spoke, it was so soft that at first Jake wasn't certain he had heard her correctly.

"I know," she said. "But he is my only family."

Jake thought of his own currently disastrous situation. His sister's death had unraveled what he had always thought of as a strong family. It was shocking how easy it was to destroy something that appeared so solid by plucking out one loose thread.

"What does your uncle do exactly, Mira?" Jake asked gently.

"I don't know," she said. She saw Jake's look of doubt. "Honest. He doesn't tell me anything. He owns a restaurant in the tenth and meets with friends and people from the homeland there. It is a bit of a local Serb hangout, but I don't know what he does. I know they listen to what he says, though. We all listen to what he says."

"I can see why," Jake said. "I met him today and he told me he'd kill me if I don't bring him…"

Jake struggled to grasp the right words. He felt the anxiety and fear of his earlier confrontation with Slava and his henchman Dragan boil up again.

"Hell, I don't even know what I'm supposed to bring him. I was so stupid, Mira!" He ran a hand through his unruly hair. There were still bits of grass in it from his earlier encounter with the sidewalk.

She reached out with a gentle hand on his knee. It was unlike her to engage in physical contact, but Jake appreciated it.

"You went and saw my uncle?" she said, her voice serious. "Why would you do that? *How* would you do that?"

"I followed Professor Schmidt to your uncle's restaurant."

"I don't understand. What does Schmidt have to do with my uncle?"

Jake pointed to the old photograph lying on the table between them, his finger just under the face of Rudolph Schmidt in the background. Mira looked closely at the photo, and then at Jake.

"This man here is Professor Schmidt?"

Jake nodded. "It would appear so."

"But this photograph was taken in Serbia twenty years ago. Why would Schmidt have been there?"

She held the photograph closer to her face.

"And he's wearing a Serbian military uniform. But that would mean…"

"That Rudolph Schmidt is actually Serbian?" Jake finished. "Yeah, I think so. Your uncle called him Zorya."

"That could be a Serbian name."

"That's what I figured," Jake said. "So Professor Schmidt is actually a Serbian who changed his name and has been hiding in Austria for who knows how long."

"But how did you get the photograph?" she asked.

He recounted his earlier visit to Schmidt's office and finding the lockbox in the desk. Jake spoke quickly to stop her interjection when he described how he took the lockbox and later broke it open.

"When I saw him in the photo," Jake said, "I decided to confront him directly. See what he had to say for himself. It was probably stupid, but I had to do something. I saw him walking from the school, so I decided to follow. That is how I ended up at your uncle's place."

"You shouldn't have gone in there, Jake. My uncle is a very dangerous man."

"Yeah," he said. "I sort of figured that out."

He recounted everything that had happened, all the way through to the face smashing and physically being tossed from the building.

"That would be Dragan," she said, her lip curling as though tasting something putrid. "He is awful. He stares at me when I go to visit Uncle."

"Yeah, I'm not a big fan of him myself."

It felt good to have someone to share his day with. For a moment he was able to divorce himself from the gravity of his situation by telling it as a story. However, as soon as he was done, reality came rushing back.

"I don't know what to do, Mira. I don't think I can go to the police. They already think I have something to do with all this."

"Did you say anything to my uncle about being my roommate?" Mira asked.

"No," he sighed. "It didn't really seem like the best time."

"That's good. He doesn't know I live with two men. He thinks I live with two other women."

"Mira…"

"I know! But he is very conservative. He wouldn't approve."

"Great. Now even if I figure out what it is he wants, he's still going to kill me."

"He won't kill you, Jake. He talks tough, but he won't do it."

Jake thought Mira didn't know her uncle as well as she believed. He'd seen enough movies to recognize the Godfather when he saw him. Slava clearly had some sort of operation going in the Serbian community that Mira was not part of. Schmidt, or Zorya, had come out of the restaurant looking roughed up—Jake knew what that was like now. Something had gone wrong in Slava's enterprise, and obviously the old man wasn't happy about it. Jake knew there was only one person who could clear it up.

"I need to talk to Schmidt. He's got the answers I need."

"Schmidt may be from Serbia, but just because he's hiding doesn't mean he is a criminal, Jake."

"It's pretty damned suspicious though, don't you think? You're from Serbia. You didn't change your name when you came to Austria."

"Yes, but—"

"But nothing, Mira. Schmidt is hiding something and I'm going to find out what it is."

"You really think he killed Christian?" Mira asked.

"I think he might have," Jake said. "But only he can tell me what is going on."

He saw her look of concern, and was touched. "I'll be careful," he said. "Schmidt is an old man. The only way he could have killed Christian was by surprising him. I won't be caught off guard. I'll be fine."

"If you say so," Mira said. "But please, Jake. Stay away from my uncle. I think he is not so dangerous as you think, but..."

She trailed off for a moment, as though even she couldn't finish the sentence she wouldn't allow herself to believe. "But Dragan is dangerous. And stupid. He might do things he *thinks* Uncle wants done."

"I understand. I will be careful."

CHAPTER THIRTY

FOR THE SECOND TIME THAT day and the third that week, Jake found himself standing outside Rudolph Schmidt's university office. Enough of playing the private detective—he would just talk to Schmidt. He would confront the man with what he had discovered, and get him to admit what he had done.

Jake knew it was risky. Although he believed what he had told Mira just a short while ago—Jake was hardly the epitome of manliness, but he would have no trouble fighting off Schmidt should things turn violent—that didn't mean the professor might not have a gun or other weapon. If Schmidt felt cornered, who knew what he would do? He had almost certainly killed Christian. He must also be behind the explosion, though Jake couldn't begin to fathom how.

He knocked loudly on the door. Jake heard movement from inside, a desk door slamming shut.

"Come back during office hours," the professor barked. "I'm busy."

Jake tried the handle, but found the door locked. He pounded on the door again, loud enough to draw the interest of those passing by.

"Professor Schmidt," he said. "It is Jake Meyer. I need to talk to you."

"Meyer?" the voice behind the door said, sounding closer. "Go away. I have no desire to speak with you."

"I'm not leaving, professor. Or should I say Zorya?"

It was silent on the other side of the door. Jake knew there was no way out of the office except through the window, as Christian had learned the hard way. After a few seconds there was sudden movement and the door unlocked. Schmidt opened just enough to show his face.

"How do you know that name?" he hissed.

"I know a lot of things. Let me in, Professor."

Schmidt looked haggard, crescent smudges of blue under his eyes. His collar was undone and his tie pulled loose. For a moment, it looked as though he would slam the door in Jake's face, but he thought better of it.

Instead, he opened the door wider and stepped to the side so Jake could enter. As soon as Jake was past the threshold, the professor slammed the door shut and locked it once more. Jake felt his heart flutter, for a moment expecting attack, but it didn't come.

The professor motioned to one of the chairs in front of his desk.

"Sit down."

Without waiting to see if Jake would follow his order, Schmidt circled around and collapsed into his own chair, his head resting back as he stared at the ceiling. Jake almost felt sorry for the man. He looked pathetic, beaten. He was far from the crisply dressed, well-heeled professor of biology that Anna had introduced Jake to just a week ago.

My God, has it only been a week? Jake thought. He glanced at his own bandaged arm and smudged pants. He didn't look any better than Schmidt at this point. They had both been roughed up by Dragan at Slava's restaurant earlier today, though Schmidt was unlikely to know that unless Slava had called.

Schmidt looked at Jake, his eyes weary and face slack.

"How do you know that name?" the professor asked again.

"Someone told me."

"Who?"

"How about you answer some of my questions and maybe I'll answer some of yours."

It suddenly dawned on Jake that he should have thought to set up his phone to record this conversation. Even if he got Schmidt to confess to Christian's death, it would just be his word against a recognized member of the University of Vienna faculty.

Too late. He would get the information and then have to convince Inspector Renner. Maybe Tess would help. Jake had no idea what he was doing; it looked so much easier in the movies.

Looking at Schmidt, he decided to ease in to his big question.

"How long have you lived in Austria?" Jake asked.

"Why do you care?"

"Just answer me."

"I've been here almost twenty-one years," the professor said.

"And you lived in Serbia before that?"

If Schmidt was surprised that Jake knew, he did a good job of hiding it.

"Yes. I was born and raised there."

"Why did you come to Austria? Why the new identity?"

The professor looked out his window, quiet now. Without turning to Jake, he spoke.

"Do you know anything about the wars that ended Yugoslavia?"

Jake was embarrassed to admit he knew very little. In many late-night, half-drunken conversations with Helmut and Mira it became clear that his education—particularly when it came to history and geography—was sorely lacking in comparison to that which the Europeans received.

"I know a little. Serbia attacked Bosnia and Kosovo. Eventually NATO had to step in, in order to help stabilize the situation."

He thought he said it with confidence. He didn't want to come off as ignorant, but Schmidt chuckled, with no humor in his eyes.

"Ah yes," he said. "The American education."

Jake bristled, despite having just been thinking the same thing. He'd be damned if he'd let this murdering bastard trash his homeland.

"Am I wrong?" Jake demanded.

"No," the professor said. "I suppose that is a very simple way to put it. But that is like saying, 'I know how God created man. He put the head on top and the feet on the bottom.' It is true, but far too simplistic."

Jake refused to be drawn in.

"So you fled the war?" he asked. "You came to Austria as a refugee?"

"I came here to start anew. The war…the horrors of that conflict…I had to escape it."

"You were a soldier," Jake said.

Schmidt looked at Jake sharply, but then relaxed his features with effort.

"No. I was a doctor."

"That may be, but you were also a soldier."

The professor gripped the edge of his desk, his knuckles turning white. To Jake it was as though he was attempting to hold himself in place.

"How do you know that?" Schmidt asked.

"I saw the photograph. Slava and two others—you in the background in a military uniform."

Schmidt could no longer keep himself seated. He jumped to his feet and Jake instinctively did likewise, knocking his chair backwards to the ground, thinking he would have to defend himself, but Schmidt backed up until he bumped into the shelves behind him. Jake almost turned to look behind himself, thinking something terrible must be there the way the old man moved from him.

"Slava?" Schmidt said. "Did Slava send you?"

"I followed you earlier today. I spoke with him."

"You did *what?*" Schmidt spat. "You idiot! Why would you do something so stupid?"

Jake ignored both the insult and the question. He moved closer to Schmidt, taking advantage of the man's obvious distress and fear of Slava.

"What happened to Christian? What did you do to him?"

Schmidt looked down to his desk drawer, the one Jake had taken his lockbox from. Jake saw the proverbial lightbulb moment as Schmidt crouched and pulled open the drawer. He pulled the files forward and saw the empty space where his lockbox should be.

"What have you done?"

"I found your box," Jake said. "I have the photo that Christian brought to you."

"Did you show that photograph to anyone?"

"What does Slava want?"

"You stupid boy. You've killed me. You've killed yourself!"

"You killed Christian!" Jake yelled before he really had a chance to process what Schmidt had said. "Wait... What do you mean, I've killed us?"

"Slava is going to kill you for that box."

"Why is he going to kill me?" Jake asked, trying hard to keep the panic from his voice.

"You Americans think you can solve any problem. Kosovo, Iraq, Afghanistan. It never ends. Your arrogance will get us both killed unless you bring my box back to me at once."

Doubt crept along Jake's spine, its icy claws taking hold. Schmidt did not appear to be bluffing; he was terrified.

"What's in the box?" Jake asked.

"You do not want to know. Bring it to me and I will try to keep you out of it. I promise."

Schmidt was pleading. He seemed genuine, his hands wringing in front of him nervously.

"What happened to Christian?"

"Never mind that," he said. "Bring me the box as quickly as possible."

"Did you kill Christian?"

Schmidt saw that Jake would not relent. He walked over to the window and looked down at the place Christian's body had fallen just days earlier. He spoke quietly, without turning toward Jake.

"That fool was going to destroy my life," he said. "And for what? For his ridiculous master's thesis. I told him as much, but he didn't care."

"Christian figured out that you were lying about your past," Jake said. "Why would he care?"

"You still do not understand. I am not ashamed to be Serbian. I am ashamed at what I did during the war. There were terrible things."

"You were a soldier. Bad things happen in wars."

"These were different. I was more than a…"

Before Schmidt could finish his sentence, a tremendous *boom* rattled the door on its hinges.

"What the —" Jake said.

As the words were coming from his mouth, there was another *boom* followed by the crack of the door's flimsy lock giving way. The door flew open and slammed into the wall, a crack spider webbing through the frosted glass.

Filling nearly all of the doorway was Dragan, still wearing the same tracksuit he'd worn earlier. A small black handgun was clearly visible tucked in the waistband of his pants.

"Dragan?" Schmidt said. "I said I needed more time."

"Slava says time is up," Dragan said, his voice deep and the words hard to understand with his thick accent.

Dragan stepped into the room and shut the door behind, the latch no longer catching properly. Was this fool going to openly attack the two of them in broad daylight in the university? Jake remembered Mira's warnings and decided not to chance it. He needed to get out of here.

Jake tried to quickly dash past the brute as he entered the room, but Dragan made up for his slow wits with quick reflexes. His hand shot out and caught Jake by the throat and began to squeeze. Jake struggled to get oxygen into his lungs.

"Slava says we only need one of you."

As he tried to see through the alternating waves of black and starbursts in front of him, Jake saw Dragan pull his gun from his waist and raise it to Jake's chest.

CHAPTER THIRTY-ONE

"DON'T BE A FOOL," Schmidt said. "Are you really going to shoot us with all these people around?"

Dragan lowered the gun and squinted his eyes, as though the very process of thinking of the ramifications of his actions caused him pain. The thug barked something in Serbian to Schmidt and laughed.

The professor responded in English. "Classes will be out any moment, Dragan. The building will be full of people."

For a moment, doubt crept across Dragan's face. He released the vice grip on Jake's throat and, with his gun hand, shoved Jake back. He turned to the door to ensure it was closed. It wouldn't lock, but it blocked the view from anyone passing by.

Taking advantage of Dragan presenting his back, Jake took a chance. He grabbed the chair he had knocked to the ground, and swung it at Dragan's exposed back. He expected it to splinter like in the movies, but instead it landed with a meaty thud. Dragan grunted in pain. Between Jake's recent rough few days and—he had to be honest—general lack of strength to start with, the impact wasn't nearly as powerful as he would have hoped.

The Serbian thug whirled around and rushed into Jake, smashing him against a bookshelf, thick copies of textbooks falling around them. Jake saw Dragan start to raise the pistol and he grabbed at it, the metal cold and foreign in his hands.

He pushed with all his might to keep the gun from pointing in his direction. Dragan hissed something in Serbian. Jake didn't understand the words, but the meaning was clear enough. *I'm going to kill you*, probably followed by a few choice curse words.

A sudden *crack* split the air, like a bolt of lightning had struck the room. A sharp stabbing pain sliced across Jake's palm and for a moment he thought he had been shot. Looking down, he realized it was only the skin of his hand being ripped by the semi-automatic's slide.

Jake had never fired a gun before—he'd never even been around one. It was so much louder in real life than it had ever seemed in the movies. He tried not to think of his sister.

Both Jake and Dragan jumped when they heard Schmidt's scream. It was a feminine yelp that didn't sound right coming from the dignified professor's lips. They both looked to him and saw him holding his stomach, dark red blood oozing from between his fingers. The professor's glasses were crunched on the floor at his feet and the man's eyes were widened in surprise.

Schmidt walked backwards until he was against the same window Christian had fallen from a week earlier. He slid to the ground, leaving a streak of blood on the glass behind him.

Even Dragan was smart enough to know when it was time to get out of Dodge. He gave Jake a sudden shove that opened a few feet of space between the two men.

"Bring the notebook to Slava," Dragan said, before turning and throwing open the door.

A few students were running away from the room, no doubt fleeing from the obvious sound of a gunshot. Dragan tucked the pistol back into the waistband of his pants and went down the stairs quickly.

Jake knew he had only moments to make a decision. The police would be here very soon. Someone must have seen Dragan run from the scene with a gun. Unfortunately, the door had been closed and no one had actually witnessed what transpired within the office. When the police arrived they would find Schmidt shot in the stomach and, by the looks of him, not likely to survive. They would also find Jake—the American international student who had been present when Christian was killed. Who had also been present when Anna was almost killed—and Jake himself, though he felt the police were ignoring that fact. And now, present when the professor he had blamed for everything lay dying. That was three strikes. Even Austrians would understand that baseball analogy.

Schmidt stared straight ahead, his eyes glassy. Jake didn't know if he was dead, but he thought so. There was nothing he could do for the man. He ran from the room, knowing he couldn't be caught here by the police. He had to talk to the authorities on his terms. Standing over a dead body wasn't what he had in mind.

Jake skipped the main stairs and went to the end of the hall, where he took a secondary stairwell. Quickly running down the four flights of stairs, he entered the building's interior courtyard before he ran through an open archway leading to the streets of Vienna. There were already three police vehicles out front, and he could hear the distinctive European bi-tone wail of others approaching.

He took slow, deep breaths and forced a walk. Jake began moving toward the city center, with no destination in mind. He couldn't go home. If somebody had recognized him with Schmidt and Dragan, the police would be there in no time. And even if no one had recognized him, once Inspectors Renner and Kurz got word of the shooting, he was sure they would be looking for him.

Scanning the busy street, Jake looked for the tracksuit-wearing scumbag Dragan, but didn't see him. He had underestimated the man. He'd thought of him only as dumb muscle, but Dragan was obviously quicker than Jake had guessed, and smart enough to avoid the police. The man probably only used two percent of his brain, but it was all dedicated to criminal pursuits.

Jake had crossed the busy Ring Road in front of the university and was in the first district of old Vienna when he heard a man's voice behind him shout.

"*Halt!*"

His mind instantly went to every old World War II film he had ever seen, Nazis barking commands at prisoners, each other, Indiana Jones. He instinctively turned to see who was yelling.

It was an Austrian police office on the other side of the road, in front of the main university stairwell. He looked straight at Jake, a heavy walkie-talkie held up to one ear as though receiving information.

"*Halt!*" the officer shouted again. A few other policemen took notice, and also looked at him. The man shouted some other words in German to his colleagues. Jake couldn't catch all of it, but he definitely understood, "*Das ist der Mann!*"

That is the man.

Jake turned and ran, blocking out the commotion from behind him, knowing all the same that they were in pursuit. A voice in his head urged him to stop running and surrender, but he quickly squashed it.

The streets of central Vienna were simultaneously perfect and awful for trying to get away from someone. Like most old European cities, there is no grid pattern. Roads curve and dead-end, centuries of construction changing the dynamics of neighborhoods. It was simple for Jake to take an almost invisible narrow alley, pass through a hidden courtyard, and find himself alone.

On the other hand, the roads are narrow and difficult to navigate between packs of Chinese and Russian tourists, and horse-drawn carriages known as *Fiaker* that care only about the tourists paying their fee and have no qualms about running anyone else down in the street. Attempting to run through these lanes, Jake felt like a salmon swimming upstream.

Don't the salmon die when they eventually get where they're going? Jake thought to himself before silencing that inner voice.

Fortunately, the police had the same problems as they ran after him. The Viennese didn't care to get out of the way, and the tourists were too oblivious to realize they should.

Jake paid little attention to where he was going. Getting lost was not his concern, only getting away from the police long enough to figure out his next move. He zigged and zagged down every other road he came across, not risking the time to look behind him to see how close the police were. He could hear angry shouts in his wake, not just from those he'd knocked aside, but also from his pursuers.

He turned left down a small road and crashed into Mozart—or at least one of the many low-paid immigrants hired as ticket touts dressed as the composer. The man's brochures flew in all directions and he shouted at Jake in Turkish.

Jake took the chance to look behind him for a moment. He had managed to put some distance between himself and the police, but he knew he couldn't outrun them forever. His only hope was to disappear.

A rack of hats stood in front of a souvenir stand. Jake grabbed a wide-brimmed hat with the Austrian red and white flag embroidered on the front. He kept running as he did so, and heard the vendor come out and shout at him.

He turned down the next road and saw a plaza opening in front of him. In the middle stood a large fountain in baroque style depicting a wedding. A large group of tourists stood around it listening to their very animated guide. They all looked up at a fake clock on the top of a nearby building.

Jake pulled the hat down on his head, slipped into the group, and looked up with them. The police came charging into the square a few moments later, and the group turned to look at them. The police looked around, scanning the crowd. Seeing only tourists, they took off down another road.

The tourists turned back to their guide.

"Well," he said. "As I was saying, we're now in Hohermarkt, or the High Market. Right where we now stand is where the old city gallows once stood. Many criminals, and probably more than a few innocent men, were executed in this very spot."

The man gave a theatrical laugh and added, "Thankfully, times have changed."

CHAPTER THIRTY-TWO

TESS WAS CAUGHT IN A Wikipedia whirlpool, clicking link after link in the online encyclopedia program. She read about the origins of the war in Yugoslavia. The conflicts in Bosnia and Kosovo. Her stomach clenched in horror at descriptions of mass rape camps and public executions. It was almost too much for her to process.

The only other time she had felt such despair for humanity was on a visit to the U.S. Holocaust Museum in Washington, DC. Photographs of concentration camp survivors, thin as baby birds, with eyes staring out blankly, and videos of corpses uncovered in mass graves had haunted her for weeks afterward. She had been there as part of a high school trip and had cried. For once, she wasn't embarrassed by her emotions and had noted more than a few other classmates and several teachers with similar reactions.

But World War II and its horrors had felt so far removed, even now, serving in Austria. There were few reminders of this horrible past on display in Vienna. The city had been damaged during Allied bombing runs and Russians fighting in the streets toward the end of the war, but one hardly knew that today, more than seventy years later.

Those were black-and-white times. It was the time of her grandparents' childhood. Hitler and his henchmen felt no more alive or real to her than Jack the Ripper or Ghengis Khan.

Reading about what had transpired in Yugoslavia, it still felt raw, the photographs in color and many of the people still alive—both victims and perpetrators. Used to American law and its common death sentences (or the strangely termed "life" sentences, which meant prison until dead), the punishments handed down to many of those convicted by the International Criminal Court in Yugoslavia seemed relatively minor: eighteen years for one; twelve for another; nine for this guy.

On top of that, many of these men (and they all seemed to be men) had never even been found. This is what worried Tess the most. What had Jake gotten himself involved in?

"G'night, Tess," Sam said as he left the office, not waiting for a response.

Her other consular colleagues were packing up around her, the work day coming to a close. She was still duty officer for another two nights, so her day didn't really have an end. Whether she sat at home waiting for the phone to ring or stayed at her desk, what was the difference?

"*Schönen Abend*," she told one of her Austrian colleagues as he passed by.

She continued clicking through articles, but went back again to the entry on the massacre at Foça. It was disgusting that somehow Professor Rudolph Schmidt had been a known acquaintance of Radyslav Pritchko—the same Pritchko who had allegedly been involved in this horror.

He wasn't named in the article, but Steve up in the FBI office had told her as much after checking his sources. Pritchko had been one of several members of a special Serbian paramilitary unit involved in terrorizing the Muslim populations. Like many of his colleagues, he had never been caught.

"We'd happily arrest him if we found him," Steve had said. "But to be honest, Tess, no one is looking too hard."

"What this man did is awful," she had replied. "He should be in jail."

"No argument here. Unfortunately, times have changed in the last twenty years and now the phrase of the day is Islamic extremists. Our radar is only so big, and these guys take up the entire screen. The last thing anyone wants is another 9/11."

Tess couldn't argue with that, but she still failed to see why the fact that there were other, possibly worse people out there, meant other bad guys got away with their crimes. *This is why I could never work in law enforcement*, she thought.

"Staying late?"

She jumped at the sudden voice almost directly behind her. Thurston had the good sense to appear embarrassed when she turned to him.

"Sorry," he said. "I didn't mean to scare you."

"It's fine," Tess said. "Probably not much later. I'm just finishing up a few things for a potential fraud case."

He raised a bushy eyebrow above his thick-rimmed glasses. "Something interesting?"

For a moment, Tess wanted to tell Thurston everything that had happened since meeting Jake Meyer: the death of the Austrian college student; the explosion—which obviously Thurston knew about, but not everything—and its connection to Jake. Most importantly, she wanted to confess to using the consular databases to look up Rudolph Schmidt, something she never should have done.

"Maybe," she said. "I'm still digging. Just an applicant with some weak ties to a wanted guy. Probably nothing, though."

It was more or less the truth, but judging by how awful she felt saying it, her subconscious disagreed.

"Well, let me know if you need any help. I've done my share of fraud work over the years."

"Thanks, I will. I'll see you tomorrow."

Thurston gave a small wave and turned to go. Tess looked around and saw she was the last person in the consular section. She shut down her computer and tidied up her work space. She hated to arrive in the morning and find things a mess. As she walked out of the front of the building, waving goodbye to the local guard, her cell phone rang.

"Tess McIntosh," she answered.

"I need your help, Tess. Things are bad."

"Jake?"

"Can we meet?"

"Sure, but what's going on?"

"Not over the phone. That place you wanted to meet before—the Bagpiper?"

"I can be there in twenty minutes."

~

The Bagpiper was in the ninth district. It was beginning to fill up. It was supposedly a Scottish bar, swords on the wall and everything, but the staff was primarily Irish. Tess guessed they figured people couldn't tell the difference. It was small and dark inside, the wood walls stained a tone darker with years of cigarette smoke. Old metal signs advertising the positive health aspects of Guinness covered the walls, with long Scottish claymores filling in the gaps. The only thing missing were any actual bagpipes.

When she arrived, about half the tables were full, along with all the spots at the bar. She found Jake at a corner high top and joined him. He looked awful. His brown curls were a mess, though it looked like he had done his best to bring them under control. She'd noticed his dark brown eyes on their first meeting, but now it was hard to see past the ugly bruise surrounding his left one. Jake's arm still had bandages from his burns, but the previously stark-white bindings were now smudged with dirt and frayed along the edges.

"You look like shit," she said in lieu of a greeting. "You should go back to the hospital."

"Thanks. It's good to see you too." His voice was scratchy, as though he'd been up all night shouting over a rock concert.

"I'm serious, Jake. You look awful. What have you been up to? Were you in a fight?"

"Yeah. Well, sort of. I went to see Schmidt."

"You fought with Professor Schmidt?"

"No. I didn't—Dragan did." The table next to them was empty, but he lowered his voice. "Schmidt is dead. At least I'm pretty sure he is."

"I don't understand what you're talking about," Tess said.

"The police are after me, Tess," he continued. "I lost them, but I think they're still looking."

"What in the hell—" Tess stopped herself short when the waiter came up to check on their drink order. She ordered a small hard cider.

"What in the hell is wrong with you?" She continued her thought after the waiter had gone, lowering her voice to a whisper. "If you killed Schmidt, then I have no idea what I can do to help you."

He stared just above her shoulder for a few seconds, as though lost in another place or another time. His eyes refocused on her.

"I didn't, Tess. I swear. Dragan shot him and ran. I ran too. I didn't do anything, but the police are never going to believe that. Too many people were in the hall. They heard us fighting inside."

Jake told her about going to Schmidt's office to confront him about the photograph. He already knew Schmidt was hiding in Austria under a false identity, and had been doing so for years. Tess tried to keep up, but Jake was jumping around, skipping details.

"Stop, Jake. Just stop. What do you mean Schmidt's name isn't Schmidt? Who is he?"

She felt a chill start at her tailbone and begin to creep slowly up her spine. Her database check on him showed him as a known associate of Radyslav Pritchko. Was he in fact Pritchko?

"His name is Zorya something. He's Serbian, and he was in their military during the war. I'm not really sure what he was hiding from, but it was something bad. This guy Dragan showed up and killed him before he could explain it to me. This is why Christian died. He figured it out."

"Zorya? Did he say anything about Radyslav Pritchko?"

It was Jake's turn to look caught off guard. He leaned in closer to Tess, and she reciprocated. This close, she noticed little flecks of green in his otherwise brown eyes. *For God's sake, Tess. Focus.*

"Radyslav?" he said. "Who is that?"

"A very bad man from the Serbian war. I've been doing some research of my own."

"Uncle Slava," Jake whispered to himself.

"What?"

"Uncle Slava," he repeated, louder this time. "Mira's uncle. He threatened to kill me today."

Tess could only imagine the look that crossed her face.

Jake actually managed to smirk. "I hadn't gotten to that part yet. It's been kind of a long day."

"If this Slava is the same man as Radyslav Pritchko, then we definitely need to call the police, Jake. This guy is bad news. He's a freaking war criminal."

Jake ran his fingers through his hair, messing up his early attempts at bringing some order to his dark locks.

"A war criminal—of course. Maybe we could just throw an axe murderer into the mix somehow."

"This is serious, Jake."

"Do you think I don't know that? I've been—"

The waiter returned with Tess's cider and a Guinness for Jake. They passed on any food. The server was discreet enough to pretend he couldn't tell they'd been arguing about something.

"I know it's serious, Tess. In the last two days I've been blown up, had my face slammed into a table, was nearly strangled, witnessed a shooting, and was chased through the streets of Vienna by the police. I understand the situation is serious."

"Okay," she said. "I'm sorry. It's just...we need help, Jake. I'm a consular officer. I do visa interviews and help people replace lost passports. This is way out of my league."

"I know." He took a sip of beer, a white mustache of Guinness foam on his upper lip before he wiped it off. "I didn't call you as someone from the embassy. I called you as a friend."

She smiled.

"Well, a friend who works at the American Embassy and may have an idea what in the hell I should do."

"I think I have an idea. Like I said, I've done some research of my own. I spoke to our FBI attaché, and he—"

"You did what?" Jake said. He put his beer down hard enough to spill a bit.

"Don't worry, I didn't give him your name. He thinks I'm working a fraud case. We can trust him, though. Maybe we should talk to him."

Jake thought about it, absent-mindedly sopping up some spilled Guinness with a napkin.

"I don't know, Tess. FBI equals cops in my head."

"He can help—I'm sure of it. This is beyond us. If Schmidt is dead…if this guy Slava is the same as Radyslav Pritchko, then we are way out of our depth. We need to—"

Jake's cell phone interrupted her thought. He looked at the screen and showed it to her. The caller display read Anna Duerning.

"Didn't you say she lost her phone?"

He nodded and answered. He didn't say anything, but just listened. What little color he had left in his battered face drained away. Without a word, he hung up after a few seconds.

"They have Anna."

CHAPTER THIRTY-THREE

"WHAT DO YOU MEAN, they've got Anna?" Tess asked. "Who's got her?"

"Slava," Jake said. "Radyslav. Whatever his name is. If it is the same guy that you're talking about. He's got her and he's going to kill her if I don't do what he wants."

"Do what?" Tess said. "This is crazy, Jake."

She didn't have to tell Jake. He knew. One day he was a student in Vienna, no troubles to speak of. Sure, he could admit to himself that he was running from his past. He was avoiding his parents. He was trying to block out the memories of his town, overrun by the media, his sister's face on television. His sister Lucy dead. Yes, there was all that.

But he had found some peace in Vienna. Between the innate beauty of the city, the tentative burgeoning friendship with his roommates, and classes he actually found interesting, he'd started to feel as though he had a place here.

And then suddenly he was Jason Bourne, except instead of having the unexpected memory of how to kick ass and shoot guns, he was burdened with all the problems of a secret agent without any of the skills to deal with them.

This was the hand he had been dealt. He wasn't going to back down, even if the very thought of facing that maniac Dragan again made him want to piss his pants. Jake hadn't been there when Lucy's life went off track. He damned well wouldn't let the same thing happen to Anna.

"Slava wants a notebook that Schmidt had," Jake said. "He wants me to bring it to him."

"Are you insane?" Tess asked. "We have to go to the police now, Jake. I know you're scared, but they'll believe you. I'll vouch for you."

"They won't, Tess," he insisted.

She opened her mouth to argue, but Jake cut her off.

"I mean, yes, they might. But it will be too late by the time we get it all sorted out. Slava says I need to bring him the book by nine p.m. or…"

He didn't want to think about what they would do to Anna. He could tell from the look on Tess's face—her research had revealed horrors Jake didn't even want to consider.

"Jake…"

"I'm serious, Tess."

He locked eyes with her. Only inches apart, they were both leaning forward in an attempt to keep the conversation to themselves.

"I have to be able to trust you, Tess. You can't go to the police. Not yet."

She took a drink of her cider and put the glass back on the table, but didn't take her eyes from the honey-colored liquid.

"Do you even know where this book is? Can you get it?"

Jake noticed she failed to say she wouldn't contact the police, but he let it go. He knew exactly where the book was, and it was clear Tess wanted to help. She was on his side, but he had to take her own safety into account. There was no reason for her to be pulled into this mess any more than she already was. Jake had a feeling Slava didn't worry too much about things like diplomatic immunity. Dragan had probably never even heard of it.

"I think I know—it's in Schmidt's office. I remember seeing something like it there when I took the photograph."

It wasn't a complete lie: he had kind of seen it in Schmidt's office. It was in the lockbox, which he'd taken from the office and which now sat underneath his bed. The book Slava wanted so badly had to be the little black diary from the lockbox. Jake couldn't understand anything in it, but it made more sense now. The combination of Schmidt's bad handwriting and Serbian Cyrillic made it a code uncrackable to Jake. He didn't know what it contained, but it was important enough to Slava to kill for.

"I don't know, Jake. It's my job to help Americans in trouble. How can you expect me to just sit by and do nothing while you risk your life?"

"I'm not asking you to do nothing," Jake said. "Just give me a head start. I promise we can go to the police together."

He covered Tess's hand with his own and gave it a little squeeze. It was cool from her glass, and he enjoyed the softness of her long fingers.

"After Anna is safe," Jake said. "Then we can go to the police."

"What is it about her?" Tess asked, her voice quiet. She looked at him for a moment, but then lowered her eyes to their joined hands.

"Anna?"

"Yeah. I mean, I'm not saying we should just throw her to the wolves, but how did this all get started? Why her?"

"I'd be lying if I said I didn't first notice her sitting next to me because I thought she was attractive." Jake noticed Tess purse her lips, and quickly clarified. "At first. But then I realized something."

She looked up. "And that was?"

"It's a long story. But remember I told you that my sister died recently?"

Jake looked up at the kitschy Irish and Scottish decor on the walls of the Bagpiper, lost in thought.

"Actually, I guess it is coming up on two years. It still feels like it just happened. It's part of the reason I'm in Vienna. It's why Mom was so quick to call when she didn't hear from me."

"I'd almost forgotten about that," Tess said. "I feel like we've known each other so long now. I forgot this all started when your mom asked me to check up on you."

"Yeah. That makes me feel pretty damned macho."

Tess laughed. It was nice to have a break from the tension, even if it was fleeting. The smile slid from her face. "What happened with Lucy?"

Jake sighed, trying not to let his mind go back to that day, or the days and weeks that followed.

"Somebody shot her."

Tess reached out and put her hand on his. "I'm so sorry, Jake."

"Somebody shot her and eight other high school students. Then he killed himself."

Tess brought the hand to her mouth. "Oh my God, Jake. Your sister was in that school shooting in Ohio?"

He nodded, but didn't say anything for a moment. "I just want to forget about the whole thing, but I can't do that. My parents are still there. There are too many questions."

"I shouldn't have pried."

"No," he said quickly. "I brought it up. I wanted to tell you. It just isn't easy to talk about, and there hasn't really been a good moment."

"No," she said. "I guess not."

"It's just…well, I realize Anna reminds me of my sister. Of what happened to her. And now that Anna is in danger, I know I have to do something."

"I get it, Jake. I really do." Tess grabbed his hand. It was warmer now, comforting. "But you're going to get hurt or arrested or…I don't know." They both knew the alternative.

"I'll be careful."

She raised an eyebrow and looked him over. He realized he was still bandaged and bruised from his last few attempts at playing the hero.

"I mean it this time."

He could tell Tess was formulating her own plan. He couldn't let her get caught up in everything. Her intentions were good, and he wanted her help badly. He was scared. He was a student, not a hero, but something had changed. As bad as he wanted Tess to help, to hope that somehow she could pull on some sort of secret U.S. Embassy resources to save the day, he knew he had to tamp down these feelings. This was the real world. She was right: people could get hurt. Christian and Schmidt had gotten killed. He wouldn't let that happen to Tess.

"You're my secret weapon, Tess."

"I am?"

"Slava doesn't know anything about you. Think about it. That is the only thing I've got going for me right now. You're the only thing I've got."

She hesitated, mulling it over. "That's true…"

Jake jumped on her hesitation.

"It is. I'll go get Schmidt's book. You go see if you can learn anything else about what's behind all this. I promise to call you before anything else happens." Jake checked his watch. There was time. "We've got a few hours before Slava is expecting me."

"You think you can get into Schmidt's office?" Tess asked.

He felt bad hiding the truth of the book from her, but he needed to get away from Tess, for her own good. If she knew the book was back at his place, she'd want to come along and it would be that much harder to keep her at a safe distance. He told himself the lie was necessary. She would understand in the end.

"I can get the book," Jake said. "I'll call you in an hour. You're going to head home?"

"Yeah," Tess said. "I don't like this though, Jake. Something doesn't feel right."

"It'll be okay. Trust me."

It didn't take a Holmesian level of deduction to see that Tess was skeptical, but he was relieved she kept her doubts to herself. It would have to do for now. He hoped everything went as smoothly as he promised. Anna's life depended on it. For that matter, Jake's probably did as well. Looking at Tess, he feared she might be in just as much danger.

CHAPTER THIRTY-FOUR

JAKE WRESTLED WITH WHAT TO do for another few minutes before he knew his mind was made up: regardless of what else was happening, he wouldn't turn his back on Anna now. Afterward, he would go to the police with Tess, and let the chips fall where they may. Now, though, Anna needed him.

He turned the corner to his normally quiet ninth-district street. At this time of evening, there should have been few cars parked on the street. During business hours a few people parked, but after hours there was almost no traffic. The buildings were either offices—mostly medical practices—or student housing. Few of the university students had cars, and the offices were closed. So why were there two plain black sedans out front and a small van a bit further down the street?

Jake stopped at the corner and took a few steps back to scope out the scene. Everything about the cars said Austrian police to him. While in the States the police liked to drive big muscle cars covered in garish decals and topped with lights, the police in Austria typically rode around in comical minivans or nondescript sedans.

Peering closer through the darkness, it seemed the cars were empty. The van was too far down the road to tell. Jake checked his watch. It was seven-thirty p.m. Slava was expecting him at the restaurant by nine p.m. with Schmidt's book, or else Anna…

It wasn't clear what Slava was going to do with her. On the phone, he had only said that he had her and to bring the book if Jake wanted to see her again. How did he even know that Slava was telling the truth? Maybe this was all a huge bluff. A trap to get Jake to do Slava's dirty work for him.

No, he thought. *Slava is not a man who bluffs.* If the man said he had Anna, then Jake believed him. After all, it would be easy enough to call or stop by the hospital and check; Slava would know that. He had to have her, and that meant Jake had to get the book. Slava must have known that after Schmidt's death, the police would be all over anything related to the Serbian soldier-turned-professor. He couldn't risk sending Dragan and having the dumb muscle get caught. Jake, however, was completely expendable.

Jake grabbed his cell phone from his pocket and thumbed through to Helmut's number. If the police were inside, Helmut could let him know. He hoped he hadn't gotten his friends into trouble.

"Hallo, Jake. Where are you?" Helmut sounded casual. Before Jake even had a chance to say anything, Helmut continued. "That sounds great. I'll have to check with Mira."

Now Jake knew for certain: somebody must be standing right next to Helmut. There was a good chance it was either Renner or Kurz. Jake would never be able to get in and recover the book with them inside. And without the book, Anna was in serious trouble. Should he just give himself up and hope he could explain everything? He looked at his watch again.

Renner seemed like a good enough guy, and Jake believed he would take the story of Anna's kidnapping seriously. After all, it shouldn't take more than one call to confirm whether she was still in the hospital. The question was whether it could happen before the 9 p.m. deadline Slava had set. What would happen to Anna if Slava didn't get Schmidt's book in time? It was too risky.

"I take it the police are standing right next to you?"

"Mm hmm," Helmut said.

"I'm outside, but I need to get inside and grab something from my room. And I need to do it fast. Any chance of getting them out of there?"

"Let me ask her."

It sounded like Helmut had pulled the phone away from his ear, but spoke loudly enough that Jake could still hear.

"He wants to know if—"

A harsh whisper interrupted Helmut. It was clear the police knew he'd be able to hear what was said. There was muffled conversation, but at the quieter volume it was impossible for him to comprehend. After a moment, Helmut came back on the line.

"Mira says she'd love to meet in the AKH for a beer. She has homework, but I convinced her to blow it off. Ten minutes?"

The old AKH, or general hospital, was now part of the University of Vienna campus. Made up of connected courtyards, it was a lively place filled with bars and shops. It was the perfect place for Helmut to lead the police. He should be able to keep them distracted there long enough for Jake to slip in and grab the book. The bit about Mira blowing off homework to join in the fun was clearly an extra hint that things were not right in the house. Mira would never blow off homework for fun.

"That'll be great," Jake said. "I'll see you soon. I promise."

"You better," Helmut said. "We'll take off now. See you in ten."

While AKH was a good place to distract the police for a while, unfortunately they'd have to walk right past where Jake was currently hugging the shadows. He decided to quickly circle the block and come from the other side of the road.

It was only early evening and there were plenty of people out and about, heading to the nearby bars and restaurants. At this point, it was mostly tourists and older residents. In a few hours, the university students would begin to take over the scene and the atmosphere would be much louder and more energetic. Vienna often felt like a sleepy city, but it truly transformed around midnight into something much crazier. Jake wasn't one for the party scene. He'd had enough drama his last few years back in the States. Now, a quiet evening in or a few drinks and discussion with friends was plenty.

As he approached the opposite corner, he moved carefully, afraid of running right into a police officer coming from an unexpected direction. He was relieved when he came to his street to find the police minivan already gone. The two sedans were still in place, but Jake assumed the rest would walk to AKH. It didn't make much sense to drive, but the van was probably more of a quick-reaction vehicle, carrying several officers. It would attract quite a bit of attention if a group of police suddenly descended on the university courtyards.

He waited at the corner for nearly a minute, staying in the shadowy doorway of a closed tobacco shop. Jake had to make certain the police had left, but he couldn't wait too long or they'd return while he was still inside. It was now or never.

At his front door, he fumbled to get his keys from the pocket of his jeans. Scratches and burns on his hand made it painful to reach into the tight pocket. Opening the door, he winced when the heavy wooden door closed, its sound echoing through the tile-covered walls of the foyer. His flat was two floors up and he took the stairs two at a time, trying to move quickly yet quietly.

He put an ear to his front door, but it was impossible to hear anything through the heavy wood. With a deep breath, he unlocked the door and went inside. Most of the lights were off, but an end table lamp in the living room still burned.

Jake moved quietly toward the room. He couldn't get to his bedroom—and the notebook—without going past the living room. If someone was there, he would have to get past them. He took another deep breath and risked the first step. Then the second. It didn't take long for him to realize there was a reason the light was on.

Mira sat at her normal seat and looked at him sadly.

"Mira," Jake said. "What are you doing here? You didn't go with the others?"

"I'm so sorry, Jake."

Her voice was barely a whisper and heavy tears pooled in her eyes, reflecting the yellow glow of the lamp next to her. Mira was almost always solemn, quiet, but he had never seen her look so sad. Jake had only a moment to realize how much more beautiful she was when she showed emotion, even if it was sorrow.

"Sorry about what?"

Mira only shook her head. "We tried, but—"

Before she could finish, the door to his bedroom burst open. Almost simultaneously, there was shouting behind him from the direction of the kitchen. Four police officers in tactical gear surrounded him, exotic-looking automatic weapons pointed at his chest and head.

The police mostly shouted in German, but Jake knew enough to throw his hands to the sky. One voice—a woman's—spoke calmly but forcefully in English.

"Do not move, Mr. Meyer. You are under arrest for the murder of Rudolph Schmidt."

One of the officers grabbed Jake's arms and forcefully pulled them behind his back and slapped on handcuffs. The police officer's rough grasp on Jake's freshly bandaged arm caused him to yelp in pain.

"Be careful," the woman snapped in German to her colleague. "He isn't resisting. We have him."

Jake finally had a chance to turn and see the woman in charge. It was Deputy Inspector Kurz, the normally silent partner of Renner. If he had ever wondered what her voice sounded like before, he wished he could have learned under better circumstances.

CHAPTER THIRTY-FIVE

THE RING ROAD IN VIENNA is regarded as one of the most beautiful stretches of architecture in the world. Tracing the former path of the old city walls, the road encloses the ancient heart of Vienna and serves to mark the boundary from the first district and the eight surrounding districts which circle it like a wagon wheel.

The evening air was crisp, with the slightest hint of decaying leaves a sure sign that fall would soon arrive. Tess loved walking the road after dark, admiring the magnificently illuminated buildings that stood as cheerful sentinels beside it. The opera house, Parliament, the city hall, the amazing complex of the Hofburg Palace, the Votive Church—each could easily serve as the star attraction for a lesser city. In Vienna, they were each but one piece of the puzzle that made the city so special.

Unlike the young lovers she passed walking arm in arm, Tess was alone, left to her thoughts. She desperately wanted to call Jake and try once again to convince him of the stupidity of his plan. Although Agent Berk hadn't told her everything his FBI files contained on Radyslav Pritchko, he had said enough to frighten her, and a few quick Google searches had filled in most of the blanks. Pritchko was a seriously bad man—the sort that historians wrote books about, and not complimentary ones. Tess didn't care that he was probably in his seventies. He was dangerous. Even if Pritchko wasn't much of a threat physically, this Dragan Jake spoke about sounded like a barely controlled attack dog. They would kill Jake without a thought.

If even half of what Tess had read about Pritchko was correct, the former Serbian officer was responsible for dozens, if not hundreds, of deaths during the fighting in Bosnia and Kosovo. What would one American exchange student's life mean when weighed against that? It was foolish for Jake to meet with Slava, even if his intention of attempting to save Anna was noble.

And I'm stupid for not doing anything to try and stop him, Tess thought to herself. Apart from her undeniable growing feelings for Jake, the entire point of her being in Vienna as a consular officer was to protect Americans abroad. How could she let him do something so dangerous?

She was passing in front of the Baroque extravagance of the Rathaus, the city hall of Vienna. In front stood a pretty park, vendors selling food and *Sturm*, a lightly fermented grape juice that was everywhere this time of year. She wished Jake was here with her. They could buy a pretzel, a few glasses of sweet *sturm*, and sit on one of the benches that looked up at the geranium-decked windows of the Rathaus.

But she couldn't. She looked at her watch. It was eight-fifteen p.m. By now, Jake was probably trying to get back into Professor Schmidt's office in order to retrieve the diary that Pritchko so desperately wanted. Tess did her best to forget that she was also conveniently turning a blind eye to an American breaking and entering.

Whether her subconscious had led her here or it was mere coincidence, Tess realized where she had walked. The wide stone steps of the University of Vienna rose before her. Tess stood at the entrance of the very place Jake might possibly be at this moment.

She couldn't let the chance slip by. She would do her job as a consular officer, as a friend: she would help Jake. Pritchko wouldn't hesitate to hurt or kill some random American exchange student. Would he feel the same about an American diplomat? She hoped not. It was their only chance.

Tess walked up the stairs and tried the front door. She was a little surprised to find it open, but remembering back to her own college days, she recalled that campus buildings were often as busy outside of class time as during. For that matter, there were probably classes still in session. On a nearby wall, she found a directory of floors and scanned it until she found the office of Professor Doctor Rudolph Schmidt listed. He was on the top floor, just as Jake had said when describing Christian's death.

She found the elevator and went to the top of the building, hoping she would catch Jake still here and that he hadn't already left for

Slava's restaurant. The elevator doors opened. The floor was dark until the lights flickered on, obviously triggered by her motion. There was no one around. This floor must be largely offices, she thought.

Tess listened carefully, but there was no sound apart from the odd bit of street noise that drifted up from outside. If Jake was here, he was quiet. She started down the hallway, checking the name plate on each door until she came to Schmidt's. It would have been difficult to miss, a stripe of plastic yellow and black *Polizei* emergency tape blocking access. A piece of paper attached to the door indicated that access was currently forbidden due to an ongoing police investigation. Below that was a paper posted by the University of Vienna administration indicating alternate arrangements for Schmidt's students. How quickly the world moved on when you were gone.

There was no sound from inside the office, and the tape stretched across the door was unbroken. Had Jake not even been here yet? They'd parted almost an hour ago—he should be here by now. Could he have somehow gotten in without disturbing the tape? Tess took another quick look both ways in the hallway and tried the door.

Distracted by the notes and police tape, she hadn't noticed the damage there. The door had obviously been smashed in and wouldn't latch correctly. It was really only a sticky police seal that kept it from swinging open. She peeled the tape back and opened the door.

The office was dark and in a shambles. It was clear a fight had taken place. Heavy textbooks were scattered about and the chair in front of the desk lay on its side. The light outside caught a crack in the window that spider webbed out from a small hole in the bottom half of the glass. Following one of the cracks to the floor, Tess first saw the dark discoloration of the wood in front of the window, a small plastic stand labeled with the number 1 sitting in the middle of the stain.

Everything became real. It was one thing to hear Jake tell the story of Dragan bursting into the room and shooting the professor, but now she could picture it.

Jake had sat there, she thought, looking to the chair knocked over. Jake and Dragan had fought there near the pile of books. Schmidt had stood there before being gunned down. His blood had slowly leaked from his body until he slumped to the floor, Jake and Dragan running to get away.

Tess needed to get out of the office. It was suddenly too small. It smelled of blood and sweat, and if she stayed any longer she was going to be sick. She ran from the room and down the stairs, not seeing the few students she passed. She didn't stop until she bolted from the front of the building back into the sharp, autumn air.

A couple of young women sat on the steps nearby, watching her gulp the fresh air into her lungs. Tess looked at them, but they quickly averted their eyes, not wanting to be pulled into her drama.

A chirping came from her purse, slung over her shoulder. It took her a moment to identify the sound and its source. *The damn duty phone*, she thought. For a second she thought about ignoring it, but knew it was useless.

"Duty officer," she said, her voice ragged and out of breath.

The Marine was too professional to mention it.

"Ma'am, this is Corporal Price at Post One," he said, his voice the same monotone staccato that all Marines employ. "I have the Austrian police on the other line. There has been an American arrested."

"Great," Tess said. "Just what I need."

There was nothing from the other end of the line, Corporal Price awaiting further instructions.

"Put him through. Thanks."

"Yes, ma'am." There was a beep and the Marine spoke again. "Sir, you are now connected with the U.S. Embassy duty officer. I am now disconnecting from the call."

Without waiting for either of them to speak, the line beeped again and the Marine was gone.

"This is Tess. Can I help you?"

"My name is Inspector Renner," a man's voice said, his Austrian accent distinct. The name sounded instantly familiar, but Tess couldn't remember why. "We have arrested an American and I am notifying you."

The language sounded a bit formal, but she understood the drill. Local authorities were supposed to notify the U.S. Embassy within forty-eight hours of an American being arrested. Some countries were better about it than others. Not surprisingly, law-and-order-focused Austria was quiet and efficient.

"Thanks," Tess said. "At this point, probably either I or a colleague will just come by in the morning to check on him."

"As you wish. He is at the central court."

Tess needed a little bit more information so she could log the call. In the morning, she would ask one of her local staff to start the paperwork and her boss would assign someone to meet the poor American prisoner.

"What's the charge?"

"Murder," Renner said calmly and without hesitation.

A chill went down Tess's spine. *You know what this is about,* a voice inside her head said.

"Name?" Tess asked quietly.

"Of the prisoner?"

"Yeah." She knew before Inspector Renner even spoke.

"Jacob Meyer."

CHAPTER THIRTY-SIX

JAKE SAT ALONE IN A cold cell. Both his bed and his seat were the same stainless steel bench that was bolted to the wall. A matching stainless steel toilet in the corner could serve as additional seating should he have guests.

The police had placed him here directly, with no conversation. He didn't understand what that meant. Certainly they had to present him with more detailed charges or give him a lawyer or something. They couldn't just leave him here, could they? As the police officer was closing the door behind him, Jake said he wanted to talk to someone from the American Embassy. He thought the man nodded, but nothing was said.

Jake had spent the last two years running from a memory, and now he was forced to confront it. He may be halfway around the world, but sitting in a jail cell in Vienna felt cruelly familiar to one in the suburbs in Ohio.

His sister Lucy had died only two days earlier, and the media had erupted. They stood vigil outside his parents' home day and night. They parked their satellite trucks, and plastic-haired reporters stood guard outside the school where Lucy and eight other students had taken their last breaths. Like maggots, these journalists had to feed, but instead of flesh, they gorged on emotion. They dug and dug until they got to the juicy red meat of sadness, fear, and despair.

It was Jake's father who had called him at college with the news. As soon as he'd answered the phone and heard his dad's voice, Jake had known something was wrong. Dad had never called him at school in the two years he had been there. As far as Jake could remember, his father had never voluntarily called someone on the phone. As a kid, it was a running joke turned serious annoyance that the man wouldn't answer the telephone even if it was ringing right next to him. The fact that it could have been a loved one in trouble didn't make any difference.

Hearing his dad's gravelly voice, Jake knew something terrible had happened. In his heart, he knew it was going to be Lucy. The small voice that lived inside him had been saying for the last several months that something was wrong with her, but he had pushed it down. He silenced it with logic and routine. Jake thought the same voice had tried to warn his parents as well, but they were just as good at ignoring it as Jake.

"Hey, Jake. It's your dad."

"What's wrong, Dad? What's happened?"

"Oh, it's just..." His father actually sounded on the verge of crying. Jake could remember his father tearing up just once in his life, and that was at the end of *Toy Story 3*. Unless Pixar had come out with the fourth in the series, something seriously bad had happened.

"Is Mom okay?"

"Yeah, she's fine. It's...I guess your sister is dead."

He said it just like that. He guessed Lucy was dead. As though the ballots were still being counted and it was too close to call. Lucy was dead. For a moment, Jake couldn't breathe. How could his little sister be gone? It just wasn't possible.

"What happened?" Jake whispered.

"They killed her, Jake," his dad said, edging closer to losing it completely. "They shot my little girl. They shot all of them."

"Who did? What happened?"

Jake got what information he could from his father over the phone and packed a bag, ready to head home. It was about a two-hour drive and he made a mental note to let his professors know in the morning that he would be away from classes.

The modern-day scourge of America: a school shooting. A horrific crime that you saw on television nonstop for a few days before the discussion quieted to a dull drone of debate that was someone else's problem. It seemed it always followed the same ridiculous loop. First came the shooting. Then the cries for gun control. The counter that more guns would have stopped the problem. Then something else shiny came along and the entire mess was forgotten until the next disaster. Rinse and repeat.

They always happened Somewhere Else. This time, though, it was his hometown. His sister.

On the drive home, he scrolled through radio stations trying to find some actual news, but in an era dominated by top-twenty stations, finding information was difficult. Cobbling together thirty-second clips, Jake learned that the shooting had taken place near the end of the school day. There were thought to be at least ten dead, one of them a teacher, and possibly four or five more in the hospital. One of the dead was the shooter, a name which hadn't yet been released.

Jake's drive always felt longer than the two hours it was. The landscape was flat and boring, endless farms stretched in either direction broken up by small towns that seemed to repeat, each with a dying city center and a rundown Dairy Queen on the periphery. Jake's own hometown was only slightly larger than these villages, and contained a wider area of fast-food options.

He grew tired of trying to find more news and switched to a classic rock station. John Mellencamp was singing about little pink houses, and Jake thought about his little sister Lucy. She was beautiful, although it had become tougher to see in the last few years. She didn't smile like she used to as a child, and the dark eye makeup made her appear more serious than Jake knew she was. He'd ribbed her a bit about her Goth phase, but she stuck with it. She hadn't spoken about any boyfriends with her family, but Lucy had been taken in by a small new group of friends that she didn't share anything about. Jake had worried, but thought she would grow out of it. Besides which, he was in college with his own life. It was his parents' job to parent, right?

One media truck already stood in front of their place when he got there, but it would soon multiply. The police and the school hadn't released the names of the victims yet publicly, but clearly somebody had spoken, eager for their fifteen minutes of fame. An insincere reporter approached Jake as soon as he got out of his car, asking about Lucy and how Jake was feeling and was he family and why did he think that this terrible thing had happened. Jake could only gape for a moment at the man's audacity and then ignored him completely and went inside.

His mom was a complete wreck. She cried openly and loudly, something he had only seen a few times in the past, like when his grandparents had passed away. His dad was holding it together, but with a silence that betrayed how upset he truly was. Jake feared the emotions were only building inside his old man, and sooner or later something like an emergency release valve was going to pop and it wouldn't be pretty.

The rest of that night and the next day were largely a blur. There were meetings with the funeral home as well as the police. A grief counselor had been arranged by some organization and his family had decided to pass for now, but promised to speak with the man later. Journalists from around the country arrived ready to shed light on the problem of school shootings; there were even a few celebrity reporters that Jake recognized. Members of the NRA, representatives from gun-control groups, and everyone in between descended, each ready to make full use of the newest stage. Lucy became just one of the ten photos that were flashed up on the screen. Actually, nine were regularly shown, the tenth—the shooter—was often listed separately, his death apparently not as meaningful.

His name was Morgan Jeffries and he was in tenth grade, the same as Lucy. He was a member of the same small circle of friends that Lucy had fallen into. When other students were asked about him, there was the near universal reply of, "Oh yeah, of course Morgan was the shooter. No surprise there." No one had ever reported anything suspicious or troubling before the shooting. He was just a weird kid who hung out with other weird kids.

It didn't take long for the media to learn that Lucy had been in the same group of friends. Why had Morgan gunned down his own friend along with the other students and chemistry teacher Abby Silver? What was Lucy doing with Morgan? There were so many unanswered questions.

There were few certainties, but the police did learn some things over the course of their investigation. One was that Morgan ended his rampage by placing the barrel of a Sig Sauer P226 against his temple and pulling the trigger. Right before he took his own life, he shot Lucy at close range, twice in the chest. What Lucy was doing with her friend was still unclear. Was she trying to talk Morgan down? Jake liked to think so, but there were alternative theories—ones he couldn't bear to hear, that had ultimately driven him to move a continent away.

These were the questions that began on the second day, and it was why the media presence outside his childhood home was especially large. Jake and his family couldn't go outside without being overwhelmed. Even inside, they had to keep every curtain and blind closed or else find a camera poking in.

It was near the end of Jake's second day back when he was pushed too far and finally decided to push back. Jake had run out of the house to grab some lunch for his family. His mom was barely eating, and after two days of crying and fasting, he was scared for her health. Dad was worthless, rarely speaking and doing his best to pretend his world had not fallen to pieces.

Jake got away from the house, but on his return a reporter from an Indianapolis network affiliate cornered him as he got out of his car, two bags of fast food in hand. The man spoke quickly, knowing Jake would escape into the house.

"Did you know Morgan Jeffries? Was Lucy Meyer dating Morgan? Did your sister participate in the shooting?"

It was a flurry of questions, none that Jake hadn't already heard whispered, but this time he couldn't let them go.

"Screw you," Jake said, his face inches from the reporter. The journalist actually smiled a bit, as though this was all a huge joke.

Before the man could follow up, Jake pushed him hard. Unprepared, the reporter fell on his ass and swore loudly. Jake hoped his cameraman had a live feed. The reporter got to his feet quickly, actually looking quite fit now that Jake was paying attention. His face was flushed, but he was trying to keep his cool.

"I'm just doing my job. Are you angry about your sister?"

It was more than Jake could take. He threw his bag of cheeseburgers in the man's face and followed up with another powerful shove. The reporter was prepared this time, and didn't go down. The camera kept rolling.

The commotion brought the attention of the rest of the media, as well as two police officers from the car stationed out front. Jake was shouting at the reporter, unaware of what he was saying. Certainly none of it was fit for primetime television. He tried to push the man again, but was grabbed by the shoulders from behind.

He shook himself loose and one of the officers pushed in between Jake and the reporter. To Jake it was just a blur of bodies and bright video lights. He had had enough. His family didn't deserve this. Lucy shouldn't have died. None of this should have happened.

Jake had never punched anyone before in his life prior to that moment, but he took a wild haymaker swing at the man in front of him. It landed solid, right on the man's jaw, breaking two of Jake's fingers and knocking the guy unconscious.

Unfortunately for Jake, he didn't punch the journalist. That would have been bad enough. He knocked out the police officer who had tried to break up the scuffle.

CHAPTER THIRTY-SEVEN

JAKE STOOD AS SOON AS Tess entered the cramped room. A small table filled most of the space; a few chairs took up the rest. He spoke quickly, before she had a chance to ask about him or find out what had happened.

"Tess, you need to tell them to let me go. Anna is in serious danger if I don't get to Slava's by nine o'clock. The guy is crazy. He'll kill her."

"I'll talk to them, Jake. But you have to start telling them the truth. You're under arrest for murder. Don't you get that?"

He sat down hard. Tess saw Jake was running on fumes. The explosion, the hospital, everything he'd been through, was clearly catching up with him. He rested his head in his hands and stared at the hard table in front of him. When he spoke, his voice was quiet, defeat creeping in at the edges.

"I know it's serious, Tess." He looked up at her. "But I haven't done anything wrong. I'll be okay. It's Anna we need to worry about."

"Do you think innocent people don't end up in prison? Two high-profile deaths at the university and your name attached to both of them. Witnesses saw you arguing with Professor Schmidt before he was shot. That's a big deal, Jake."

"Those same witnesses also saw Dragan smash into the room."

"That may be, but the police don't have Dragan. At least not yet, but they do have you."

Jake slammed his fist down on the table, and grimaced in pain. "That's why they need to let me go. If I can get Anna free, I can tell the police where Slava's restaurant is. Dragan will be there. Everything will be better."

"And why do you need to go? Why not just send the police?"

"Slava is waiting on me to bring Schmidt's book. If he sees the police show up, what's to stop him from just killing her? I have to go, then I'll tell them everything."

There was a certain logic to it, but Tess knew the police would never let him go. She looked at her watch.

"Even if I could get the police to release you—which I can't—you can't make it, Jake. Fifteen minutes? It isn't possible."

"Fifteen minutes?" Jake asked. "Shit!"

He got to his feet and paced back and forth, rubbing his face as he thought. He was mumbling quietly to himself, but Tess couldn't catch the words. He began to frighten her. Jake seemed on the verge of losing it.

"You need to sit down. You have to tell the police, Jake."

Tess circled the table and put a hand on his shoulder, stopping his pacing. She waited for him to look at her. He looked tired, but alert.

"It's the only way now," she said.

"No," he said. "Let me use your phone. I can still save her."

"Who are you going to call?"

Tess looked around the room, expecting the police to come in at any time. She wasn't sure how long they'd give her with Jake. She was still new at this sort of thing. In her time in Vienna, she'd only met with a few arrested Americans, and most faced minor drug charges. She'd certainly never had to visit someone on such serious charges as murder. The police typically treated the consular visit similar to an attorney visit and allowed a bit of privacy, but there was nothing that said they had to. They could come in at any time.

"Just let me use your phone. I have to call Slava. I have to tell him what happened."

"You just want to call the war criminal in hiding and ask to reschedule?"

"War criminal? What are you talking about, Tess?"

"I tried to tell you before, but you were too hyped up to listen: I've been doing some research of my own. Radyslav Pritchko is an international fugitive wanted for war crimes during the wars in Yugoslavia. This is bigger than just Anna. The authorities have been looking for this guy for years."

"So we sacrifice Anna for the greater good? Is that it?" Jake yelled. He jerked away from Tess's grasp. "I can't do that, Tess!"

Tess could feel the flush building in her face as her own anger mounted. "Quit thinking only about yourself for a minute," she snapped, moving to position herself in front of Jake.

"Myself? I'm trying to save Anna. I don't know what—"

"No, you're trying to be the hero. You're trying to make up for whatever happened to your sister. This isn't a game, Jake. This is serious, and we need to let the professionals handle it. Pritchko is responsible for the deaths of dozens, maybe hundreds, of people. I'm sorry your friend got mixed up in it, but we have to look at the bigger picture."

Jake was very still and quiet. Tess worried she had gone too far by bringing up his sister. She didn't know what the story was there, but it was definitely something Jake was still grappling with. His mother too, if the phone calls were any indicator. Tess knew she was right, though. If Jake had listened to her at the Bagpiper, if they had gone straight to the police then, maybe they would still have time to try and rescue Anna. Now? If Pritchko was prepared to go through with his threat to hurt Anna, it didn't seem like there was much they could do to stop it.

Jake sat on the edge of the table. He appeared to physically deflate, all of the fight draining out of him.

"Will you at least let me call Pritchko and try to stall him? Then I'll tell the police everything."

Tess looked at him and pulled her embassy-provided cell phone from her pocket, but didn't hand it over.

"You promise?" she asked.

Jake nodded, but didn't make eye contact. It was as good as she was going to get. She felt bad for hurting him, but she hoped one day he would understand.

She gave him the phone and he quickly dialed a number.

"How do you know the number?" she asked.

"I don't. I'm calling Mira." After a moment, he spoke. "Mira, it's Jake. I…there's no time for that. I need your uncle's phone number. I will explain it all later."

Tess could hear Mira's voice on the end of the line, her pitch rising.

"I'm under arrest, Mira. I can't go there, but I need to talk to him. I need to stall him. Just give me the number and I promise to explain. I won't mention you."

Jake mumbled some number over and over to himself as he hung up and immediately dialed.

"It's Jake Meyer."

Tess couldn't hear the other end of the call, other than a muffled man's voice. She should have told him to put it on speaker, but who knew how Pritchko would take that.

"I know…yeah, I've got it, but there's trouble." Jake stood, his agitation forcing him to move. "I just need a little more time. I'll get it to you… Don't you touch her! Let me talk to Anna."

There was a slight pause, and Jake's tone changed drastically—it became softer, comforting. The voice of a big brother, Tess thought.

"Everything's going to be okay, Anna. I will see you soon and—" He stopped, and when he spoke again his tone changed abruptly. "Yes. I understand."

Even Tess could hear the sudden shriek that came from Anna through the phone. It was quickly cut off, and again she heard Pritchko's mumbling voice.

"You son of a bitch!" Jake shouted. "If you touch her again I'll kill you!"

Jake nodded even though Pritchko obviously couldn't see it. He had a look of determination that Tess hadn't seen from him before. She had the feeling he had made a decision—a decision that she wouldn't be happy about.

"I'll be there. You bring Anna."

Jake hung up and returned Tess's phone, but didn't say anything. Whatever the plan was, Jake didn't seem eager to let her in on it.

"Well?"

"I bring him the book, he gives me Anna. That's the deal."

"We need to talk to the police now, Jake. You tell them where the restaurant is and they'll save Anna. She'll be there with Slava. Everything will be okay."

Tess hoped she sounded more convincing than she felt. It would be dangerous. If Slava saw the police were coming, it was impossible to know what he would do to the girl. He, or at least the violent thugs he kept around him, were capable of anything. But what was the alternative? Send Jake in alone for the handoff, like he was in some sort of Tom Cruise movie? At any rate, the police would never agree to let him go for something so risky.

He was quiet, and his silence hurt Tess. It was obvious he felt betrayed. She didn't know where their relationship had been heading, but she might have just sent it crashing into the rocks. Rescuing a damsel in distress from a wanted war criminal made for a terrible first date. Though Tess had to admit she'd had worse.

"Go get Inspector Renner and tell him I'm ready to talk." Jake's voice was barely above a whisper. "I don't think there is much time."

Tess put what she hoped was a comforting hand on his upper arm. "She'll be okay, Jake."

CHAPTER THIRTY-EIGHT

AS THE DOOR CLOSED BEHIND Tess, Jake knew he had only seconds to act. This was by far the stupidest thing he had ever done. Considering some of the actions he'd already taken in the last week, that was saying something. There simply wasn't enough time to wait for the police to take action. There would be serious repercussions to his life, he knew. He might even go to jail, but at least Anna would be safe. She had to be.

Jake cracked the door to the interview room and watched Tess walk away, looking for Inspector Renner. This wasn't Riker's Island, San Quentin, or one of countless other prisons that Jake learned about through wasted hours watching prison reality shows. This was Vienna, Austria, and he was in what was generously described as a minimal-security environment. Prisoners must never try to escape here, but Jake had taken note of the lack of security as he was walked to the interview room. He wasn't even handcuffed. He knew if he acted quickly and confidently, he could walk right out. Time to put the theory to the test.

Although late in the evening, the building was busy. Uniformed police as well as many others wearing simple street clothes walked about. Jake had gone by the building countless times, and though he didn't know the specifics, he thought it was also a courthouse.

In the hall heading the opposite way from Tess, Jake walked with purpose, but at a normal pace in order to avoid suspicion. As long as he didn't cross paths with Renner or Kurz, he should be fine. No one else was likely to recognize him, but just to be safe he snagged a red windbreaker jacket that someone had left on the back of their chair.

Throwing it on quickly and pulling the sleeves down to hide his bandaged arm, Jake entered the stairwell and went down.

It was almost too easy. Fate hadn't been a friend to Jake this last week. Really, fate hadn't been on his side or his family's for almost two years now, it seemed. But tonight, maybe she was ready to throw him a bone.

The front entrance area was busy and Jake hesitated. Should he try to move quickly through the crowd and out the front doors in the cool Vienna night, or would it be better to find a side exit and take more time navigating the building? Deciding time was more precious, Jake entered the busy lobby and nearly bumped right into the back of Deputy Inspector Kurz. Fortunately, her back was to him and Jake swerved at the last moment toward the front door.

He didn't risk looking back to see if Kurz had noticed. If she had, he'd find out soon enough when she raised the alarm and everyone swarmed him. At least, that was how it played out in his mind. In reality, no one said anything. No one paid attention to yet another young man as he walked out the front doors of the local courthouse and to the freedom of the streets of Vienna.

CHAPTER THIRTY-NINE

THE STREET IN FRONT OF Jake's apartment was empty, the cars he'd earlier guessed as belonging to the police no longer in sight. The walk to the apartment had been tense, not only because at any moment he expected the police to descend upon him, but also because he feared they may still be at his home, going through his belongings looking for evidence. Fortunately, neither fear proved founded.

Unfortunately, it wasn't until he was at the front door to his building that Jake remembered he didn't have any keys. They, along with his wallet, cell phone, and everything else from his pockets, were still at the police station. Security may not have been at the highest caliber, but they knew enough to check a suspect's pockets before locking him up—or leaving him unattended in an unlocked room, as the case may be.

He buzzed his apartment hoping that either Helmut or Mira was home. It was the first time he had given much thought to his roommates during this insane day. Apart from the earlier phone call, Jake felt he hadn't seen or spoken with Helmut for the longest time, but in reality it had only been a few hours. And Mira...well, Jake didn't know what to think. Had she turned him into the police? She must have, or why apologize right before they swarmed him? Why would she have done such a thing when it was Mira who had sent him looking for the very photograph that had drawn him deeper into this web of danger and ghosts from the past?

Soon, Jake would have his chance to ask her.

"Yes?" Mira's voice was hesitant over the intercom. They rarely had visitors during a weeknight and the day had already been a crazy one.

"Mira, it's Jake. Let me in."

For a moment there was only silence, and Jake feared she would refuse him entry. He considered his options. It would be easy enough to break the glass on the front door and let himself into the building, but his apartment itself would be tougher. He might be able to climb the fire escape, but Jake had never been great with heights. Luckily, it didn't seem it would come to that—the door clicked open just when he was sure he'd run out of options. Jake entered the building.

When he got to his floor, the door was open and Helmut and Mira both stood in the doorway. Helmut's bulk took up most of the space, but Mira was taller and could be seen over his shoulder, her hands up to her mouth as though seeing a ghost.

"Jake, they let you go?" Helmut asked as Jake approached.

"Let's talk inside." He pushed past them and into the apartment. Neither of them resisted his entry. That was at least promising.

Jake went to the living room and turned to see Helmut locking the door back up. Helmut came closer, but Mira hung back in the shadows.

"I don't have much time," Jake said. "I only stopped by to grab something from my room and then I'll go. The less time I spend with you guys, probably the better."

"What do you mean?" Helmut asked. A moment passed and his eyes widened. "Did you escape? Please tell me you didn't escape."

"No, not exactly," Jake started. "Well, yes…I mean technically, but I didn't have any choice. I'll turn myself back in once Anna is safe."

"Are you insane?" Helmut asked. "They think you killed the professor."

"I know," Jake said. "But I didn't."

Helmut and Mira looked at each other. He could feel the unspoken conversation between the two of them. They had already discussed the topic and passed judgment.

"I didn't," Jake said with more force. "Dragan did it, but I was there. People saw me there."

Helmut came forward, his arms up and palms facing Jake. "We know, Jake. We know you didn't do it. We think the police even know, but they need you to get to this man Dragan."

Jake looked to Mira, strangely quiet this entire time. Was she in agreement with Helmut?

"Do you believe me, Mira?"

He could see the inner battle she was waging, one between friendship and family, honor and integrity. Her expression softened and she stepped forward into the light of the living room.

"I do, Jake. If Dragan was there, then I have no doubt he would kill Schmidt. Dragan is no better than a chained dog, ready to strike when his master commands."

"And that master is your uncle," Jake said.

When Mira didn't answer, Jake went to his room and found the lockbox under his bed where he had left it. Opening the lid, he grabbed the cheap black diary. He didn't understand the gibberish inside, but to Pritchko it had clearly been worth killing for.

"What is that?" Mira asked from the doorway. Helmut stood beside her, also trying to see into the room.

"What this is all about, I guess. Your uncle says I need to bring this to him or else Anna will pay the price."

Jake sat on the edge of the bed, the diary in his hand. Mira avoided his gaze, but he wouldn't let up.

"He'll kill her, Mira. The same way he did Christian. Yes, maybe he didn't do it personally, but do you honestly believe he isn't behind Christian's death? Don't you want to see him punished for what he has done?"

She swallowed a heavy sob and abruptly left the room, knocking Helmut to the side as she did so. Helmut watched her leave with a look of confusion.

"Why do I feel like there is a lot more going on than I know about?" he asked.

Jake sighed. Helmut had been nothing but a friend during all of this, and he had returned the favor by ignoring him and keeping him in the dark. He deserved to know.

"Mira was seeing Christian. Not recently, but before."

"What are you talking about? No she wasn't…"

"She was, Helmut. She kept it from you because she didn't want to hurt your feelings." Jake said it as kindly as he could.

"Hurt my feelings?" Helmut said, following with his trademark belly laugh—this one obviously forced. "Why would she think it would hurt my feelings?"

"You should talk to her, Helmut. Tell her how you feel."

"I don't know what you're talking about."

"I think you do," Jake said. "But I'll leave that to you. But let me tell you from experience, you never know what the future holds. Don't wait until it's too late."

Helmut chewed his lower lip, but didn't speak. Jake hoped his friend would eventually find the courage to share his feelings with Mira. Jake wasn't sure what would come from it, but there was no sense in keeping it bottled up. Sooner or later, it would have to be confronted.

Jake wished he could take the time to talk more, but it couldn't be now. He had to meet with Slava and give him the book if he was to save Anna. Certainly the police would have noticed his escape just minutes after he left the station, and they would be looking for him. His apartment would be one of the first places they went. He had to get out of here.

Mira's bedroom door was closed and she didn't answer his knock on the door.

"I'm going to meet your uncle, Mira. I know you want to protect him and he is your family, but you need to eventually pick a side. He's dangerous. You need to tell the police what you know."

He was greeted only by silence. Jake knew she could hear him, and he hoped she listened. Whatever hold Slava held over her was clearly strong. He didn't know if it was only familial loyalty or something else, but his roommate clearly feared her uncle just as much as she loved him. Jake wondered if she'd always had suspicions about his dark past, but was only now forced to confront it.

Helmut stood nearby, lost in his own thoughts.

"The police will be here soon," Jake said. "It's probably best to be honest with them. I was here. I grabbed something from my room and then I left. You didn't know I escaped. Tell them that and you will be okay."

"This is crazy, Jake."

"I've been hearing that a lot lately." He said it lightly, hoping to defuse a bit of the tension, but even jovial Helmut appeared stressed. "It'll be all right. I've got to do this."

Helmut nodded and held out his hand, and Jake took it. He didn't like the feeling that this was goodbye. Jake certainly hoped that wasn't the case. Goodbye meant either he was in prison after this for a crime he didn't commit, or his meeting with Slava and Dragan had gone terribly wrong. Neither was an option he wanted to consider.

"Good luck, Jake," Helmut said. "Don't worry about Mira. I'll talk to her."

Whether Helmut was referring to Jake's departure or whether his friend would finally share his feelings, Jake wasn't certain. At the moment, he didn't have time to find out.

As Jake walked out the front door, Helmut called after him. "Where are you going? To the restaurant?"

"It's best you don't know. It'll be easier with the police. Tell them whatever you need to."

Helmut's look of concern crept into Jake's mind as he walked from his building into the cool darkness of the Vienna night.

CHAPTER FORTY

AS SOON AS TESS SAW the empty room, she knew Jake had tricked her. He probably saw it as some gallant act of chivalry. He would not only save Anna, but keep Tess out of it. To her, it was the kind of reckless act that would not only get Anna killed, but probably Jake as well. To top it off, if the police decided she was involved in his escape, she'd probably lose her job, or worse.

"Where is he?" Inspector Renner asked. He looked to Tess, expecting an answer to his question.

"I don't know. He was here when I left him."

"*Scheise!*" Renner swore before yelling something in quick, clipped German that she couldn't follow. Whatever he'd said, it had an immediate effect as commotion erupted in the hallways.

"He can't have gone far," Tess said. "How could he get out of the building?"

"Miss McIntosh," Renner said, his English becoming worse with the strain of the situation. "This is Vienna, not...Fort Knox. We do not have bars and locks and guys with big guns on every corner."

It was an odd choice of reference she thought, but it didn't seem like the time to question him. Obviously, he was right. She had never visited a jail in the States before, but somehow she guessed they had considerably more security than she had seen in this building. Even the jails in Vienna seemed to go more for aesthetics than practicality.

It was time for Tess to make some tough decisions. She couldn't deny that she was developing feelings for Jake—feelings she thought he might share. But what he was doing was stupid. This wasn't a movie, and he wasn't the hero. Radyslav Pritchko was a deadly man. If Jake thought he could save Anna on his own, she feared he was making a terrible mistake. If she allowed herself to be mercenary about the situation, his so-called concern for her safety was likely to get her fired.

"I think I know where he has gone," she said to Renner. "But he's trying to help. He didn't kill Schmidt."

"I know you want to help this man," Renner said. "And, between us, I do not think he killed the professor, but—"

"You don't think he killed Schmidt? But why did you arrest him?"

"*But*," Renner continued sharply, cutting her off. "He is the only lead we have. Arresting him was the only way we could be certain he would not leave Austria." Renner held up his hands as though to ward off blows from Tess. "It was not my decision. We all have bosses, Miss McIntosh."

She saw his logic. Even Jake had admitted he was at the scene of the crime when Dragan killed Schmidt. If Pritchko had managed to live as a ghost all these years in this city, the man was very good at hiding. Jake was their best chance at capturing him.

"Where did Mr. Meyer go? I want to help him. I promise you that."

Tess believed him. Despite his somewhat gruff appearance, she found she liked the man. He struck her as honest, and a twinkle in his eye betrayed a bit of the sly Austrian humor she had detected in many of her colleagues at the embassy. Perhaps it was simply his ridiculous little mustache, but Renner made her think of her childhood watching old reruns of Agatha Christie's *Poirot* on PBS.

"He's trying to save Anna. What he told you is true. This man Radyslav Pritchko has kidnapped her."

"And how does he expect to help her? How does Mr. Meyer propose to outmaneuver this man who has hidden from the world for twenty years?"

It was clear Renner had done his homework. Whoever finally bagged Pritchko would have quite a prize and the accolades that went with it.

"I'm not entirely sure. Schmidt had a book—a diary of names, I guess, and now Jake has it. Pritchko is desperate to get it."

The petite detective that was often at Renner's side appeared in the doorway. She was slightly out of breath. A bit of sweat sparkled on her brow, serving to make her only more attractive, Tess noticed with a bit of disgust. She looked at Tess pointedly and then to Renner.

"It's okay," he said in English.

"We are still looking," Kurz said in flawless English. "But so far there is no sign of him in the building. We've locked down so if he is here, we'll find him."

"Somehow I do not think he is still in the building," Renner said, turning to Tess.

"No. When he sent me for you, he must have been planning to run. I let him call Pritchko with my phone and—"

"You did what?" Renner came as close to a shout as she'd heard. Even Kurz jumped slightly.

"All right, it wasn't a good idea. I see that now, but I believe him about Anna. Pritchko would have killed her if he didn't get the book by nine p.m. Jake just wanted to stall him and then he said he'd tell the police how to find him."

"And what did they discuss?" Renner said, trying to regain his typical calm.

Tess felt a flush come to her cheeks. Recalling the earlier events made her feel like a teenager caught coming in after curfew.

"I don't know. They agreed to meet later in the evening. The book for Anna—that's the deal."

"He's going to get himself killed," Kurz said. "Pritchko cannot let him or Anna live."

It was direct and to the point. Kurz was right, and they all knew it. Had Jake come to the same realization, or was he too naive to see it? Would he risk everything to save Anna to make up for failing to save his sister?

Renner ran his finger and thumb along his mustache, thinking out loud.

"A man wanted for more than twenty years finally appears and the only person who can lead us to him is missing. This is not good. Not good at all."

"Wait," Tess said. "Jake isn't the only one who can lead us to Pritchko. I know someone else."

~

Mira sat stone-faced on the couch, Helmut on the arm next to her, his hand on her shoulder to offer comfort, though she didn't acknowledge him. Heavy blue smudges under her eyes and frazzled bits of brown hair escaping from her ponytail were a better reflection of her emotions than her lack of words.

Renner sat across from her, Kurz and Tess standing off to the side. As soon as they had arrived at the apartment, Mira seemed to know where these questions would lead. Whether she was prepared to be helpful had yet to be determined.

"Miss Vladic," Renner said. "We do not have much time. We must know where your uncle's restaurant is. Your friend Jake is in great danger, as is another woman. You can save them."

"At the expense of family."

"Your uncle has to answer for his crimes, but we can stop him from committing more if you help us." Renner's voice was calm, but firm. "He has done many bad things. He might well kill your friend Jake."

Mira finally looked to Helmut, sitting next to her. He nodded, squeezing her shoulder gently. "Think about Jake. And Christian."

She sighed and looked at her hands, clasped tightly in her lap.

"I swear I didn't know about my uncle's crimes," Mira said quietly.

"No one is blaming you —" Renner said, but she cut him off.

"I am not trying to defend myself. I know my uncle is a bad man. I did not know his specific crimes, but I know he has a dark past. You must understand, though, from where I came. Many did things they are not proud of. My own mother..."

She didn't finish the sentence, and no one prodded her. Time was slipping away, but they all knew that pushing Mira would not help. As they spoke, Jake could already be meeting with Slava.

Mira took a deep breath.

"When my mother died, Slava was all that I had. He paid for me to come to Vienna. I did not even know he lived here until last year. He appeared without warning, that terrible man Dragan with him." Her lip curled at the name. "There were many like Dragan back in Serbia. Tough men who cared only about drinking and fighting and the glory days of Serbia."

"Dragan will pay for his crimes," Renner said. "But first we must find them. We have to do it fast. Jake is already in danger."

"My uncle has a restaurant in the tenth district. It is near Saint Anton's Church."

Renner immediately got to his feet as Kurz dialed someone on her phone. At this time of night, Tess knew it would take ten to fifteen minutes to get to that part of Vienna. Hopefully, other officers who were closer could assist.

"They will not come peacefully," Mira said as they were leaving. "My uncle will not give up to you. And Dragan will do whatever it takes. He will fight you."

Renner nodded, and they left the apartment. Tess hoped they would be on time.

CHAPTER FORTY-ONE

NOT FAR FROM THE UNIVERSITY of Vienna on the Ring Road stood a city institution. Café Landtmann was arguably the most famous of the renowned cafés of Vienna—with only its historical rival Café Central vying for the crown. Within the wood-paneled halls of the café, tuxedoed waiters served both locals and tourists alike a mix of traditional Austrian foods as well as exquisite coffee drinks, the recipes perfected over the last one hundred and fifty years.

While Landtmann had historically catered to the upper crust of Viennese society—Sigmund Freud had regularly pondered upon the meaning of dreams over a *Doppel Brauner*—Café Central had been the home of the proletariat revolutionaries, from a young Hitler and Tito to Stalin and Trotsky.

Like any good tourist in Vienna, Jake had been to Café Landtmann previously, but also like a true university student he was hardly a regular, with its expensive menu selections and hoity-toity atmosphere. He had been surprised when Radyslav Pritchko had told him on the phone that they would meet here at ten o'clock instead of at Slava's own restaurant. However, with Tess listening in carefully, he hadn't been able to question the man on it. For her own protection, he didn't want her to know where the meeting would take place. It was the only way he could be certain she couldn't follow. He hoped one day he would be able to make her understand, but a heaviness in his stomach told him he had burned that bridge. He hated it, but he had to do it for Anna—and for Tess herself, though he knew she wouldn't see it that way.

Unlike the traditional American idea of a café, the Viennese versions were open late into the night and just as busy in the evening as they were in the morning. An older man in a perfectly spotless yet poorly tailored tuxedo greeted him at the door.

"I'm meeting someone," Jake told the man, not bothering with German. He knew the waiters at Landtmann would all speak English, even if they didn't want to admit it.

The man nodded and proceeded to ignore him. Jake scanned the room. With the rich mahogany of the walls, it was dimmer inside than one would expect considering the brilliant chandeliers overhead. He saw Pritchko sitting in an upholstered booth in the far corner. He could have been any elderly tourist from Eastern Europe. A plain button-down white shirt was open far enough to reveal a golden orthodox cross hanging from a chain around his neck. More noticeable to Jake than any token signs of religious affiliation was the person who sat with Pritchko. No one. No Dragan and, more importantly, no Anna.

Jake approached the table and sat across from the man without waiting for an invitation. If Pritchko was bothered by this, he gave no indication. He pushed a menu toward Jake.

"I recommend the *Fiaker*," Pritchko said, his voice pleasant. "You can get them anywhere in Vienna, but they do them the best here. Just the right amount of rum."

"I'm not interested in any goddamn coffee, Slava," Jake said, without looking at the menu in front of him. "Where is Anna?"

Ignoring his question, Pritchko beckoned a waiter over. In flawless German, he ordered.

"We will have two Fiaker, please." He looked to Jake. "Anything to eat?"

Jake shook his head and bit his tongue. Pritchko knew he had the upper hand. Causing a scene wasn't going to help Anna.

"Nothing to eat, then," Pritchko told the waiter. The man left to enter their order.

Jake could feel the diary in the back pocket of his jeans. He felt stupid now for bringing it inside. Clearly Pritchko had more experience in this world. Jake knew he was out of his league. He opened his mouth to speak, to demand to know where Anna was, but Pritchko beat him to the punch.

"Your friend is safe enough. She will stay that way as long as you do what you were told to do. Do you have the book?"

Jake didn't know what to say. If he admitted he had it, would Pritchko uphold his end of the bargain? He realized then that he should have listened to Tess and involved the police.

Before he could answer, the waiter returned with their drinks. As with every café in Vienna, the table was quite small and even the simplest of orders came with multiple little plates, glasses, and dishes. By the time the waiter finished setting their two coffees, glasses of water, some bread, honey, and jam on the table, there was barely a free spot between them.

"How do I know you will let Anna go once I give you the book?" Jake asked as soon as the waiter left.

Pritchko gave his coffee a little stir and took a sip, the foam giving him a momentary mustache of white. The image was hard to reconcile with Tess's information that the man was a wanted war criminal, or Mira's insistence that her uncle was a dangerous man. Jake had learned not to underestimate him, though.

"What good is the girl to me? All I want is the book that this fool Zorya was keeping."

"What's in the book?"

Pritchko slammed his cup of coffee down hard onto the saucer, a bit of froth spilling over the edge. His face reddened.

"That is no concern of yours! Do you have the book with you?"

As suddenly as the storm had erupted, the man returned to his former calm. "Your friend is safe. But I'm afraid my friend Dragan is not known for his patience. The longer she is alone with him…"

He let the threat linger in the air. Jake felt his stomach turn at the thought of Anna alone with the vile tracksuit-wearing goon.

"What happens after I give you the book?" Jake asked.

"I call Dragan and he lets her go. A simple exchange." Pritchko said it so casually that for a moment Jake almost believed it could be so easy.

"Call him first and tell your dog to let her go. When Anna tells me she is safe, I'll give you the book."

For a moment, Pritchko was silent. He gave his coffee another stir and then a big gulp. Jake thought the man was weighing his options. Certainly one of them might be to kill Anna and him both the moment he had the chance. In fact, it was probably high on the list. Jake wished he had his phone. If he could call Renner or Tess, maybe the police could move in while he had Pritchko distracted. Of course, that was assuming Anna and Dragan were back at the restaurant. They could be anywhere.

"Very well," Pritchko said suddenly. "But let me see that you have the book with you."

Jake hesitated, but the old man followed up.

"I am hardly going to wrestle it away from you in the middle of Café Landtmann, am I? A young, strong man such as yourself?"

Jake doubted that Pritchko had any qualms about resorting to physical violence, even at his age, but it was true he was unlikely to do so in such a public location. With that thought in mind, Jake reached into his back pocket and pulled out the black diary. He held it up with one hand, out of Pritchko's reach.

"This is it?" Pritchko asked.

It was clear to Jake that it was an honest question—Pritchko had obviously never seen the book in question. If Jake had known that from the start, he could have brought a fake.

"This is the only book Professor Schmidt, or Zorya, had."

He brought the book back down to his lap. "Now call Dragan and tell him to let Anna go. He gives her the phone and when she tells me she is safe, the book is all yours."

Pritchko narrowed his eyes as though looking for alternatives, but then pulled a small cell phone from his jacket pocket. It was a cheap Nokia. Jake guessed the man probably changed phones regularly in order to avoid detection. Pritchko hadn't managed to remain a fugitive from the world's police for the last twenty years by being careless.

Keeping his eyes on Jake, he dialed. After a moment, he quietly said a few words into the phone that Jake couldn't understand.

"It is done," Pritchko said. "Go across the street to the park in front of the Rathaus. Dragan will give her to you."

Jake didn't like it. He knew the park Pritchko was speaking of. There would still be people around at this hour, but it was large enough and dark enough to feel isolated. It was not a safe place to be alone with a killer like Dragan.

"Why can't he bring Anna here?" Jake asked.

"Because the police are looking for him. Now give me the book."

The book felt heavy in his hand, though in reality he knew it weighed almost nothing. Giving it to Pritchko meant the man probably would continue to walk free despite the horrible crimes he'd committed, but adding the death of Anna to the list wouldn't help. Jake slowly slid the diary into his front shirt pocket.

"You and I are going over together," Jake said. "I'm not going over to face that psycho alone. You're going with me. Once I have Anna, you can have the book."

"That was not the deal," Pritchko said, his voice quiet but heavy with menace.

"I'm changing it. I'm tired of being pushed around. My rules now."

Pritchko was silent. After a moment, his eyes narrowed. Jake was sure that if the old man thought he could get away with stabbing him at that moment, he would have.

"It is about time you grew some balls," Pritchko said. He dropped a twenty-euro note on the table and stood. "Let's go."

"She'd better be safe," Jake said. If the old man was intimidated, it didn't show.

"Go," Pritchko said. "You'll get your little friend and I will never have to see you again."

As they left Café Landtmann, Jake worried about the different ways he could interpret that statement.

CHAPTER FORTY-TWO

ALTHOUGH WELL INTO THE NIGHT at this point, a surprising number of people still walked the streets in the tenth district. Young Turkish immigrants, women pushing strollers, and old men on park benches discussing the Old Country filled the plaza around the grandly restored St. Anton from Padua Church. On a nearby corner stood the unmarked restaurant of Radyslav Pritchko, just as his niece had described.

Tess was grateful that Renner and Kurz had agreed to bring her along, even though she had no real business being here. The Regional Security Officer at the embassy would be seriously pissed if he ever learned. She hoped that he wouldn't, but it seemed certain tonight's events would be making the local news whatever the final outcome. If all went well, a fugitive for twenty years would finally be in custody and junior officer Tess McIntosh played a small role. If things all went to shit…well, Tess preferred not to think about it.

A special response team of Austrian police had parked nearby and were already on the scene by the time Renner, Kurz, and Tess arrived. The SWAT unit was wearing Kevlar vests and carrying small submachine guns. They looked ready to fight. Renner and Kurz had only their normal business suits, but had small pistols in hand.

"You will stay in the car," Renner told her. "Do not get out until I tell you otherwise."

Tess wanted to argue, but had to admit that underneath the adrenaline, she was scared. She had never been around so many guns, and she couldn't imagine bursting into this restaurant. From what Jake had told her of the man Dragan, it was likely he wouldn't give in without a fight. He had killed Professor Schmidt and had to know he would go away forever if caught.

From the sedan, she saw the SWAT unit come at the front door from both sides, the officers careful to avoid exposure to the windows. More police had arrived on the scene and were keeping curious bystanders back. The man that seemed to be the leader of the tactical squad stood next to the front door and yelled commands in German. From fifty feet away the words were still clear to Tess.

"*Polizei*! Turn on the lights and lay down on the floor!"

For a moment there was nothing. Tess thought she just couldn't hear the answer from where she was, but judging by the tense posture of the police, they had yet to receive a response. In Tess's mind, she pictured Dragan shooting Jake and Anna and preparing to take on the police. She shook her head to chase off the horrible images.

Tess rolled down the police car window so she could hear better. *It isn't as though the glass is going to do much to protect me if bullets start flying,* she thought.

The squad leader shouted the same instructions again. This time, he ended with a threat. "We will shoot!"

For a second, there was nothing. Then a frightened woman shouted something from inside the restaurant that Tess couldn't understand. It sounded like German, but in her agitated state, the words were unclear. The squad leader answered, quieter this time.

After a moment, the front door opened and a young woman with raven-black hair and pale skin walked into the police spotlight. A SWAT member grabbed her roughly and pulled her toward a nearby police car. The rest of the team continued their vigil outside the restaurant.

Tess saw Kurz go over to speak with the frightened woman they'd pulled from the restaurant. The woman was crying, but Kurz did nothing to comfort her. The squad leader made a motion with a closed fist before counting down silently with his fingers. Three. Two. One.

The team exploded into motion. Three officers darted into the front door while others near the window covered them through the glass. Tess heard shouts from inside the restaurant, but they sounded like the well-coordinated barks of police jargon rather than voices of panic one would expect from a fire fight.

After a few tense moments, the lights came on inside the restaurant and the squad leader came back out through the front door. He walked over to Renner. The two spoke for a moment, and Renner nodded. There was a noticeable diffusion of the tension as the tactical squad lowered their weapons and started chatting among themselves, as though it was just another day at the office. For them, Tess figured it was.

She got out of Renner's sedan and walked toward Kurz and the woman from the restaurant. She saw Inspector Renner going in the same direction.

"Dieter," Kurz said. "You're going to want to hear this."

Dieter, Tess thought to herself. *So he does have a first name after all.*

Deputy Inspector Kurz turned to the woman and motioned to her partner. "Tell him what you told me."

The woman was young, but clearly tough. Her tears from the terror of moments earlier had dried, leaving only streaks from her heavy black mascara. She furrowed her brow, clearly angry that she had spoken to the police. She didn't want to speak again, but Kurz was also tough and didn't back down.

"Tell him now or you are going to jail," Kurz said.

The woman stared hard for a moment at Kurz. After a quick glance and subsequent dismissal of Tess, she turned to Renner.

"They aren't here. The meeting isn't here." The woman spoke German, but with a Slavic accent. *Serbian as well*, Tess thought.

"We see that," Renner said. "Where did they go?"

For a moment it seemed she wouldn't continue, but Deputy Inspector Kurz grabbed her arm roughly. If Renner was bothered by his partner's style, he showed no indication.

"Rathausplatz," the woman spit. "They're meeting in front of the Rathaus."

"And Jake?" Tess said, ignoring the look from Kurz. "My friend is meeting them?"

The woman finally acknowledged Tess. She looked at Tess from head to toe and then laughed.

"Another stupid American? Yes, your friend meets them there. He will meet Dragan. Then he will see he is not as tough as he thinks he is."

Tess turned to Renner, but he was already ahead of her. He barked commands to the police around him and they loaded their vehicles. Others got on radios to redirect resources to the Rathaus. It was a large area, and they needed to surround it to be certain Pritchko and Dragan didn't escape. More important to Tess, they had to get there before Jake got himself killed.

A uniformed officer came and grabbed the Serbian waitress and began to take her to another police car. Before they were gone, Tess had one last question.

"What about Anna? Is she still safe?"

The woman laughed, but without any hint of warmth. "Safe? Oh yes, your little *plavojka* is quite safe. We take good care of her."

The way the woman spoke chilled Tess. These people were monsters. She hoped it wasn't too late to help Jake.

~

It was strangely normal standing at the crosswalk waiting for the light to change. Radyslav Pritchko, murderer, rapist, war criminal, stood by Jake's side. Still, it was Austria and the stereotypes about the Germanic world and their love of rules didn't come from nowhere. When the walk symbol turned green, Jake and Slava crossed from Café Landtmann into the dark park in front of the Rathaus. Jake knew that somewhere in the poorly lit paths and among the statues commemorating Austrian heroes he had never heard of, waited Dragan and Anna.

Slava walked slowly, befitting his age, but with purpose. It didn't feel like a bluff. Slava clearly knew where to go. If Jake was walking straight into a trap, there was little he could do about it now. He'd chosen to do this without the police—he had no one to blame but himself. Jake only hoped that by throwing in the last-minute kink of forcing Slava along, he could create enough of a distraction to allow a safe escape with Anna.

Jake's mind whizzed through possibilities as they walked, desperately hoping to think of something that might allow the two of them to get away. His brain kept running through scenarios showing him as the hero—grappling with Dragan, disarming him, and holding them for the police. Jake didn't think any such heroics were likely to prove successful. A far better plan was to wait for Anna's release, throw the book, and run like hell. It might be cowardly, but given the circumstances, he'd take it.

Despite the late hour, Jake had hoped to find more people in the park, but was sadly disappointed. The plaza in front of the Rathaus was home to countless festivals throughout the year, most stretching late into the night. It was his bad luck to be here between the yearly circus, but before the Christmas market. There was almost no one around.

After a few turns in the dark, they approached a bench in a particularly shadowy corner of the park. Jake could make out Anna sitting and Dragan standing behind her, one hand resting on her shoulder and the other discouragingly out of sight. Jake knew the man would have the same pistol he'd killed Rudolph Schmidt with at the ready.

"Dragan," Slava called as they approached. "There has been a small change in plans."

"Yes, boss," Dragan said, clearly unconcerned. He wasn't the brains of this operation. Whatever Slava had planned would not affect Dragan's role.

"Our friend Mr. Meyer does not seem to trust us. He would like Anna first. Then he will give us the book."

Anna looked down at her hands. She and Dragan still stood about twenty feet away, but Jake could hear her sniffling, upset.

"It's going to be okay, Anna. Everything is fine."

He tried to sound confident, but was sure none of the four of them bought his false reassurance.

Slava chuckled next to him, and Jake felt his stomach tighten. The man was too sure of himself. Jake sensed no fear at all from the old man.

"Oh, yes," Slava said. "I am certain everything will be just fine." The man smirked as he spoke. Jake didn't like the man's arrogance. Was this all a show?

Something was wrong. He tried to ignore the feeling. *Just do the exchange and run.* The busy street wasn't more than one minute away. If he and Anna could just get there, they would be safe. Dragan wouldn't dare follow them. He would go to the police and tell them everything. Anna would talk. Their names would be cleared and the police could arrest Slava and Dragan back at the restaurant.

The restaurant that Jake and Anna both knew about.

Slava and Pritchko knew he knew.

They couldn't let Jake out of this alive. It hit him hard, and for a moment he couldn't breathe. They were never going to let him or Anna leave this park. Soon Tess would be receiving another call—this time about the death of an American in Vienna.

It was the image of Tess taking that call that pushed Jake to action. He grabbed Pritchko by the arm and held him in front as a shield. If Dragan was going to shoot, he'd have to do it through his boss.

The man struggled, but was old and clearly used to having others do his dirty work for him.

"What in the hell do you think you're doing?" Pritchko growled.

Dragan pulled his other hand up and pointed the gun Jake had known would be there. He hoped the man wasn't too good a shot. At least it was no longer pointed at Anna.

"Watch it, Dragan! Anna, get over here behind us."

She finally looked up. In the shadows it was tough to see her expression clearly, but a bit of moonlight caught the tears in her blue eyes. She looked so sad.

"I'm so sorry, Jake."

For a moment, it was Lucy's face looking back at him, tears streaking her makeup, her lip trembling. Had his sister known what was going to happen to her? Did Anna know? Jake didn't want to fail again. He tensed himself and prepared to lunge.

Then, the world around him exploded into noise and commotion. Police came from multiple directions at once, and the red dots of laser sights bounced around on all of them. Voices in German shouted directions, but all Jake could understand was "Down!" and "Gun!"

Dragan slid his hand from Anna's shoulder and grabbed a fist full of blonde hair. He yanked her to her feet, a scream slipping from her lips. He held her close to his chest and pointed his pistol at the side of her head. Her feet were barely able to touch the ground, the bench between her and Dragan knocking at the backs of her knees.

At the sudden movement, nearly all the red dots quickly swung over to Dragan. The shouting intensified. Jake saw Inspector Renner off to his left, focused on Dragan.

"Let the girl go," he said calmly. "Nobody has to be hurt."

Jake knew Dragan would never surrender, probably not even if Slava ordered it, which seemed unlikely. Police officers had forced Jake and Slava to their knees, their hands above their heads.

"Renner," Jake shouted. "He'll kill her. Tell your men to put their guns down."

As if to emphasize Jake's concerns, Dragan yanked harder on Anna's hair and she cried out in pain.

"I shoot her!" he said.

Jake could feel the officers tense around him, all waiting for what came next.

"Drop your gun," Renner commanded again.

"It's going to be okay, Anna," Jake said from his knees, hoping to reassure her. "Dragan, don't do this."

For a moment, time stood still for Jake. The sounds of the police quieted to a dull roar and Dragan's incomprehensible Serbian shouts were nothing more than a steady drone. Anna looked at him with the big soulful eyes that reminded him so much of his sister. It seemed she spoke quietly, just for him, though later he realized everyone must have heard it as well.

"I'm so sorry, Jake," Anna said again. For the first time since he'd met her, not so many days ago, Anna looked serene, at peace. Gone were the shadows that had haunted her pretty eyes whenever he spoke with her.

Releasing her hold on Dragan's hand clutched in her hair, Anna grabbed his pistol. It happened so quickly it was impossible to tell her intention. Jake liked to think that she tried to force the barrel of the gun to the sky, where it would fire harmlessly. Some might have speculated, though not to Jake, that she forced him to pull the trigger and took herself from the equation. What happened next, though, was clear to everyone present.

The loud snap of the Glock split the night air, shocking Jake with its volume. A spray of blood burst from the side of Anna's beautiful straw hair and she slumped in Dragan's grasp. Almost instantly, the well-trained Austrian police responded to the gunfire and returned with shots of their own. Dragan's torso and head were peppered with bullets and he fell face first across the bench and over Anna's already-crumpled form.

CHAPTER FORTY-THREE

JAKE SAT ONCE MORE IN the same interview room he'd fled just hours earlier. He noticed they had posted not one but two uniformed guards outside the door. If nothing else, he'd helped the Austrian police fix a glaring security flaw.

Tess was across from him, her hands over his handcuffed ones. She looked tired and much happier to see him than he deserved. He had treated her like shit. He understood that, but had told himself it was only to keep her safe. Seeing her again, he realized how foolish he had been. He had almost lost her, lost everything, and now was forced to process what she was telling him.

"Schmidt killed Christian?" he asked. "So I was right."

"It seems that way," Tess said. "With the professor and Anna both dead, it is hard to know for certain, but Slava has been talking. He's not so tough now that he's alone and behind bars."

"But how does Slava know?"

"Schmidt supposedly told him. Christian was asking too many questions. It was going to lead to Slava eventually and ruin Schmidt's insurance policy."

"The book?" Jake asked.

Tess nodded. "Schmidt had too much dirt for Slava to touch him, but then the professor made the mistake of going to Slava for help."

Jake had a splitting headache and trying to follow Tess's story was becoming increasingly difficult. After a second, it hit him.

"The bombing?"

Tess nodded again. "Schmidt believed Anna knew the truth about Christian's death. He needed her dealt with." Tess was quiet for a second, clearly holding something back before deciding to push forward. "Once Anna involved you…"

"I had to go as well."

"That was the plan," Tess said, and smiled at him. "It's a good thing you're tougher than you look."

He laughed. "Is that supposed to be a compliment?"

"Just don't let it go to your head. And, as a representative of the United States, please promise me you'll avoid all war criminals in the future?"

Jake held up his hands. "No promises. I haven't registered for next semester's classes yet."

She laughed again. Jake could get used to that sound. As terrible as everything had been the last few weeks, meeting Tess was definitely the silver lining.

Before Jake could say anything else, the door opened and Inspectors Renner and Kurz entered. Kurz said nothing, but unlocked Jake's handcuffs.

"Does this mean he's free?" Tess asked. "I mean, I'm asking as his consular representative."

"Yes," Renner said, his lip twitching in a slight smile. "I'm sure. Yes, Mr. Meyer. You are free to go, though we still have plenty of questions for you."

Jake rubbed at his wrists, trying to restore blood flow back into his hands. "You finally believe that Dragan killed Schmidt?"

"We always believed that, but the gun collected tonight matches the ballistics."

"You should have come to us immediately," Kurz said. "It was stupid not to."

"Yeah," Jake admitted. "It probably was. I'm still confused, though. So Schmidt killed Christian?"

Renner nodded, fingering the end of his little mustache. He seemed to relish the role of that Agatha Christie sleuth, pulling together the loose ends.

"And I know Dragan killed Schmidt."

"Clearly," Renner said.

Jake realized all he wanted was to go home. His head was throbbing. He had burns on his arm from being nearly blown up just a few days earlier. And, come to think of it, he'd missed nearly every class for the last week. Leaving the drama of his shattered home behind hadn't worked out as well as he'd hoped.

"Is there anything else I can help you with?" Jake asked.

Renner and Kurz traded looks. He saw a hint of a smile on Renner, but it wasn't reciprocated by Deputy Inspector Kurz. Jake thought he'd never get on her good side.

"No," Renner said. "I think you have done quite enough, but in the future, Herr Meyer?"

"Yeah?"

"Please leave the capturing of international fugitives to us?"

"You got it."

~

Jake, Tess, and Helmut sat around a worn wooden table at the Bagpiper. Jake and Helmut were on their second Guinness, while Tess continued to nurse her cider. The room was smoky and loud and the normalcy of it all was refreshing to Jake.

"That's crazy," Helmut said as Jake finished telling his story from the night before. Helmut had heard some of it, but never start to finish and not with Tess's portion filled in. "All I did was study for my British history exam."

"Don't even talk to me about schoolwork," Jake said. "I've probably already been booted from half my classes."

"Well, since many of the professors think you killed one of their own, you might have a little more pull than you think." Helmut laughed loudly at his own joke, and Jake winced. He hadn't even thought about the kinds of stories that must be floating around.

"How's Mira doing?" Tess asked Helmut. "First Christian, then her uncle…"

"It's not her fault," Helmut said, a bit too quickly. Tess pulled back, and he noticed. "Sorry. I guess I'm just a bit defensive on her behalf. She knows that a lot of this revolves around her in one way or another and I think she's just processing it all." He looked to Jake. "You know how she is."

"Yeah," Jake said, though he knew very little of what went on in Mira's head. He hoped his friend would get through this. He worried she might leave Vienna altogether and start someplace new. Helmut would be heartbroken.

They were all quiet for a moment, each lost in their own thoughts. It didn't last long before Helmut broke the silence.

"Enough of this sadness. It is time to look forward. So…with that." Helmut raised his glass and waited for the others to follow suit. "I propose a toast. To putting this all behind us."

"To Anna," Jake said, hoping no one had noticed his voice choking up a bit. If they did, they were kind enough not to acknowledge it.

"And to Christian," Tess added.

"And to…" Helmut started, and paused for dramatic effect. Jake knew his roommate was a consummate comedian, but if he even mentioned Dragan, he might have to dump his Guinness over his friend's head. Perhaps sensing the tension, Helmut finished.

"To friendship."

"To old friends," Helmut motioned toward Jake.

"To new friends," he motioned toward Tess, who smiled back at him.

"And to something more than friends," Helmut said with a not-so-sly wink at both Jake and Tess.

"Hear, hear," Jake laughed as he clinked his glass with Helmut's and then with Tess.

She locked eyes with him and smiled. "Hear, hear."

THE END

Afterword

Thank you so much for reading. If you enjoyed the book, it would mean a great deal to me if you would consider doing two things.

1. Please take a few minutes to leave a review on Amazon. For indie authors like myself, reviews and word of mouth are crucial to our success. Your help goes a long way toward the future success of my books.

2. Choosing to publish independently comes with many benefits, but there is no denying it is much tougher to get the word out. Because of that, I've started a mailing list for my readers. In addition to be the first to learn about new releases, I'll be doing giveaways of exclusive bonus material. And I promise, no spam.

Go to www.shawnkobb.com for more information.

About the Author

Shawn Kobb is an American author living in Vienna, Austria. In addition to writing mysteries and thrillers, he moonlights as a diplomat and has lived and worked in Ukraine, The Bahamas, Afghanistan, and Washington, DC. If he told you any more than that, he'd have to kill you.

Before joining the U.S. Foreign Service, he worked as a 911 dispatcher for a large city in the Pacific Northwest well-known for its rain. Not Seattle, the other one. While working as a dispatcher, he had ample opportunity to develop plot ideas while speaking on the phone with crime victims, murderers, naughty children, and schizophrenics.

He lives in Vienna with his wife, a dog, and a cat.

12965435R00116

Printed in Great Britain
by Amazon.co.uk, Ltd.,
Marston Gate.